Alan Robertson

MAN'S WORK

outskirtspress
DENVER, COLORADO

Outskirts Press, Inc.
http://www.outskirtspress.com

ISBN: 978-1-4787-3353-9

Outskirts Press and the "OP" logo are trademarks belonging to Outskirts Press, Inc.

From Dude !
to Dude !

Al

# MAN'S WORK

# One

**"Zim, why you** s'pose some folks never do crime while others can't seem to stop?"

Billy Jardean, serious and innocent, sandy-blond hair and handsome blue eyes set in a billboard cowboy face, looking older than his twenty-eight years from too much sun and bad nutrition. He was rarely introspective. Maybe it was the killing that put him in the mood. Maybe not. He wasn't the kind to get into it that deep.

Rolling north along I-75 through the heartland of Michigan, knee on the wheel, Zim Crenshaw used both hands to scratch at a three-day growth, skin underneath red and itching, hoping he hadn't picked up ringworm during his brief stay in the one-cell lockup. Tall and lanky, with a narrow face, hawk-nose and angry black hair that couldn't be controlled without grease or spray, chronic skin problems and self-professed to be bright, he was the polar opposite of Billy.

Zim clamped his hands on the wheel. "Couldn't say.

Ain't had much experience with work. Tried it once, but
it didn't feel right. I'm not what you'd call a morning
person. Know what I mean?" He glanced at Billy to see if
he was listening. Satisfied, his eyes returned to the road.
"Can't stand alarm clocks. Don't like any kind of clock."
One hand drifted to his cheek to take care of a problem
area as he segued into philosophy. "Time. Huh! Fuck's
that? Nothing. Can't touch it. Can't see it. Can't smell
it. Hell, time's a nuisance. You're hungry, you're hungry.
Don't matter what *time* it is. You want eggs and bacon?
Don't matter if it's midnight. Yes, Billy, time puts you in
a prison. It's a prison of *time!* Some boss probably came
up with it just to get you to work harder."

Billy nodded at the wisdom.

Zim was primed. "No. A man like me ain't cut out for
work. And if you ain't cut out for work, that only leaves
bumming and crime. And bumming's got way less going
for it than crime. Plus, someone's gotta do it, otherwise
the system would break down, crumble, collapse, you understand what I'm sayin'? We're playing a vital role in
the scheme of things. We're makin' it happen."

Billy frowned. "My stomach knows what's happening. Knows I'm hungry."

Zim nodded. "Let's pull over next side road and see
what gramps and grammy have in the way of disposable
income. Tell 'em our 401ks are underperforming, test
their sense of charity."

Billy shrugged a yes and glanced at the Glock inher-
ited from the dead deputy at the Podunk sheriff's office.
Zim getting out of Ionia recently and right away jump-
ing parole—plus him already being down twice—meant

he'd be swapping butts for Grecian Formula before the
door swung open on the B&E charge in Gaylord. The
cop caught him in the damn house for chrissake! Wasn't
like some D.A. was gonna plead it down to a walk. Plus,
they'd been cellies for a year at Ionia. Had to do it.

They drove the deputy's personal car—a cherry
'66 Mustang—south to the first rest stop, reluctantly
abandoned it, then jogged across I-75 to the adjacent
northbound stop and, to their delight, found two oldsters
about to climb into a silver Caddy after taking a whiz.
There was no one else around.

Driving past Gaylord, Zim and Billy were efferves-
cent, reasoning that after the cops found the Mustang
they'd concentrate their search to the south while the dynamic duo were driving north and west.

An hour later they left the lush farmland of Lower
Michigan behind, crossed the five-mile suspension bridge
over the choppy Straits of Mackinac, and then turned left,
motoring westward into slanting rays of afternoon sun
in the general direction of Bemidji, Minnesota, where
Zim had buds he hoped would bunk 'em till the heat died
down.

They followed US 2 as it snaked along the northern
shore of Lake Michigan. Sandy beaches and blue water to
the left, thick pines to the right. Light traffic, easy driving.

The old couple was still kicking and banging on the
trunk. Not as much now, since it'd been nearly two hours,
but Zim could still hear their muffled shouts and it pissed
him off. He took the first right, drove a mile into nowhere,
pulled to the side. "Let's do it."

Zim unlocked the trunk. Billy to his right, two steps behind, relaxed, Glock in hand, ready for business. As the lid flowed upward, Zim too stepped back. He appreciated good maintenance. The smooth movement of the lid made the moment more enjoyable.

Lying on spotless beige carpeting, the wrinkled pleats of the old man's face pulled into a tight scowl. "You fucking pricks!" He struggled to right himself. "I'm gonna kick your asses all the way to Green Bay!" He slowly swung one arthritic leg out of the trunk and then the other, unknotting the muscles with veiny hands. Billy thought it was pathetic, wanted to cap him right there, put an end to his misery.

"You two shit monkeys oughta be ashamed of yourselves," piped the old lady, voice ragged from age and shouting. The musty squawk a doll from the attic makes when you step on it. She'd been farthest in and did a slow half-roll into the open before pushing herself up. Way she was dressed—all buttoned up with white frills—looked like the kind who spent half her life in church, yet her language created a troubling disconnect in Zim. He scrunched his face in distaste. She went on. "Picking on old people. Jesus! Don't you have any fucking pride?"

Zim was nonplussed, eventually managing, "Lady, you got a mouth on you."

Billy was struggling with the interpersonal dynamic. She sensed weakness and turned on him. "What are you staring at, asshole? Thinkin' maybe you'll get some?"

Christ almighty! She was about a hundred years old. 'Getting some' was absolutely the last thing on his mind. He closed his eyes, recoiling from the thought.

The man was fully out now, helping the woman over the edge of the trunk. "I suppose you punks think you're gonna rob us and leave us here."

Zim and Billy both nodded.

"Fat fucking chance." He glared at Zim. "You caught me by surprise at the rest stop. Try me now, asswipe." His left foot shuffled forward, a fighting stance. His right hand slipped into his suit pocket and came out with a switchblade, handle dancing blue and green, glittery, high-quality mother of pearl, a real work of art. He thumbed the button and a six-inch blade shot out, snapped into place, razor steel glinting in the cold September sun.

Zim's mouth hung open in disbelief. "Are you fucking crazy! Empty out your pockets before I get pissed off."

"Tell him to gum your wood," said the old lady.

"Yeah," said the old man. "And gimme my keys right now or I'll carve you into a hundred chunks of shit."

Zim turned to Billy. "There's just no reasoning with some people."

# Two

After dragging the bodies far enough into the woods so they wouldn't be seen and stripping them of their valuables, Billy used the old man's handkerchief to blot the blood splatter from the trunk and bumper and they were off. A map from the glove compartment informing Zim the town of Manistique was less than twenty miles away. The dot telling him it was big enough to have a toilet. Maybe a place to eat. They were both real hungry.

As Billy drove, Zim rifled through the booty. The old man's driver's license gave his name and address as Victor Vanko, 5 Chipmunk Lane, Loon Haven, Michigan. Hmm . . . Loon Haven. Zim gave it some thought. It was late in the day. He wanted a shower. Wanted desperately to scrub his face. Wanted food, smokes, booze and a warm place to sleep—not suck down a couple jummies and crash half-sweaty, half-cold in the damn car, stumble outside at three A.M. to take a leak with a billion sand flies gnawing on his dingus. It was another long day of driving to Bemidji and the Caddy weren't no sipper. The coots had a hundred twenty in cash. Take every damn penny just for gas. "Billy, you got anything on you?"

"Two bucks is all." He kept his eyes on the road. "We spent the rest at the bar before you got popped." Billy was a conscientious driver, obeying speed limits and making full stops.

Zim said, "Appraising at our finances, I'd say we got just enough to pay gas to Bemidji. Blow twenty on breakfast and we won't make it without hittin' something along the way." He spread his hands in a gesture of acquiescence. "I'm all for doin' crime when the need arises, but ain't no sense in leaving a trail of crumbs to the cabin. Know what I mean?"

Billy didn't but nodded anyway. He'd learned young that when confused it was better to say nothing and nod. Better than being made fun of for not knowing and then to having to kick the shit out of someone, which he really didn't mind doing, but too much and you run out of friends. Better to nod. His stomach ached. "I'm hungry, Zim."

"Me too, Billy, but look here what I'm sayin'. Those old farts have a house in Loon Haven. Map says it's only an hour and a half from here. We got a car now, so all we need is food and a place to sleep and tomorrow night we're partying in Minnesota." Zim's face fell. "Damn! Now that I think of it, we're gonna need more money anyway. My friends in Bemidji are charitable, but they ain't rich. Know what I mean? Considering the circumstances and all, they'll be expecting us to bring 'em a gift to offset their risk. I'm sure they'd prefer dope, but cash or some easy to fence substitute would do just fine."

Billy didn't quite grasp the point, zoning halfway through, but he nodded. It was identical to the previous nod.

"What say we man up and drive through to Loon Haven? Spend the night in geezerville. Hit the fridge and watch TV. They probably got booze, too."

Hungry as a wolverine, Billy's time horizon had compressed to substantially less than an hour. Maybe twenty minutes, max. Impulse control had always been an issue. "Man, don't you think we oughta eat first? What if they got neighbors outside and we can't get in till dark? That's a couple hours. I don't think I can wait."

Zim knew Billy was fixated on eating at the earliest opportunity, which would be Manistique, and he reflected on the fact that thwarting Billy's desires had not been prudent enterprise for others. Physically, they were about equal, Zim being taller and rangier, a better boxer, but Billy had muscle on him, workouts and 'roids, difficult to discourage. And Zim knew getting into a fair fight was always a mistake, especially with the only friend he had, so he came up with a compromise.

"You got a point, Billy Boy. Let's stop in Manistique, fill our bellies, and snatch a twelve-pack for the road. Take care of our current needs now and let the future worry itself. We can still spend the night in Loon Haven. Maybe the geezers got money hid under the mattress or stashed in some pathetic wall safe. Jewelry for sure."

Billy smiled. Zim smiled too.

Hunger slaked, a frosty can of Blue Ribbon in his hand as they rolled northward away from Manistique toward Lake Superior, Zim said, "Vanko . . . hmm . . . rings a bell."

"Vanko's a common name," said Billy, a bump causing a geyser of beer to shoot from the can nestled between his legs, soaking his pants, making it look as though he'd peed.

Zim gave him a sideways glance, mouth puckering in embarrassment. The boy was ignorant but had a good heart. Zim was older, forty, felt protective. "Yeah, common, but unusual too." He put his shoulder to it, "Vanko, Vanko," straining to rip a byte of memory loose from the pinched grip of brain cells tight with desire for serious alcohol and any of a wide range of pharmaceuticals. "Vanko . . . hmm, ever hear of Mad Dog Vanko? Big time mobster out of Chicago. But that was when I was a kid."

Billy shook his head. He wasn't much for history. Not even crime history. He had trouble remembering things.

"Heard he disappeared. Mad Dog Vanko."

After shoplifting a Loon Haven street map from a Chevron station, they discovered Chipmunk Lane was five miles west of town. The sun was dipping low, the clouds pink and purple sand dunes. An arching sign over the entrance proclaimed, *"The Pines."* Newish blacktop leading to sizable lots. Five, ten acres apiece. Road curving through manicured forest. Underground utilities. Classy shit. Money. Zim and Billy were ecstatic.

They saw it on the left about a quarter-mile in. Wooden sign hanging from a beam across two posts. Picture of a sailing ship in relief over rough blue ocean, 5 carved above, Vanko below. Curving paved drive. Already dusk.

No one around. Lots so big you couldn't see the other houses. Couldn't even see Vanko's from the road.

"Drive in?" queried Billy, slowing the Caddy to a walk.

"Got no alternative, Billy Boy, 'cept sleep in the car. Don't want that."

Billy nodded. Made the turn. The Glock was lying between them on the seat. Zim picked it up, casually, without any complicated thought, like a carpenter might pick up a hammer. "We have the key, so it's easy. Lights off, we go inside. Lights on, we play it by ear."

"Sounds right," said Billy, admiring Zim's ability to plan on the fly, but when the trees opened onto an expansive lawn fronting a massive home, all plans were off.

"Looks like we just hit pay dirt, Billy Boy." Shit-eating grin on Zim's face.

Billy's mouth hung open in disbelief as he stared at the two-story behemoth of dismal gray stone, a hundred feet wide and half as deep, Frankenstein windows across the front, a gaudy stone cornice, hordes of gargoyles, sinister towers at each end, and a battlement of ugly teeth ringing the roof. In the center, up a set of stone steps and across a stone porch was a heavy wooden door with a wrought-iron knocker. The house was dark. A circle drive led to the entrance. Billy cruised to it and shut off the engine.

Zim said, "Let's do it."

They climbed the steps and Billy used Vanko's key to open the door. Zim stepped in, Billy behind him. The entryway was dark. Zim found a light switch, and when he clicked it on, their eyes opened in wonder. They were standing in a large wood-paneled foyer bedecked with Medieval paintings, grim tapestries, and a real suit of armor.

"Cool!" said Billy.

Zim stayed professional, alert, moved forward. On his left was a staircase leading to second-story bedrooms. On his right was an arched entryway to the great room. Beyond it, a hallway stretched left and right. A kitchen lay straight ahead.

"First things first," whispered Zim. "I'll check the upstairs, you check down, make sure no one's home." Glock in hand, he moved toward the staircase. Zim having the gun made sense. If a house is dark and someone's in it, they're probably in a bedroom, maybe with their own gun. Accepting his role, Billy casually strolled from room to room on the ground floor, lighting each as he went, taking a glance inside, and then moving on. Opening the very last door of the very last room at the end the very last hallway, he heard someone catch a breath. "Zim!" he called. Billy stepped inside, searched for the light switch, found it, flicked it on. Eyes blinking. "Zim! . . . you better come look what's here."

# Three

**B**illy **was in** a small blue windowless room. In front of him, sitting on the edge of a single bed, was a young woman. Thin, twenty maybe, straight black hair to the middle of her back, pale white skin, large dark eyes. She was wearing a maid's dress like in movies. Black and white. Short. The way it hung on top, it didn't seem like she had a bra on, or needed one. Billy thought it was kinda sexy. Kinda weird too. She was staring at him, alert, didn't move a muscle. Billy called again, this time with more urgency. "*Zim!* I need you to come here!"

Billy never had much to say and rarely raised his voice, so Zim knew whatever it was was important. Cruising downstairs at full throttle, he poked his head in every room on the ground floor until he arrived at the very last room at the end of the very last hall. Striding in, his eyebrows went up. "Jesus! What we got here?"

Billy eyed him, not speaking, seemed obvious.

Zim gnawed on the inside of his cheek. "Shit." He

stared at her. "What's your name?"

Her waiflike eyes came to life. She

An accent. European. Russian.

"Where you from?"

"Chicago." The word pronounced chick-ah-go.

For Zim, hearing the name of that particular city gave rise to a disquieting feeling. He pushed against it and moved on. "You Russian?"

"Ukrainian," she replied, a rolling, guttural sound to the r. "I spit on Russians."

"That's good to know." It got him thinking about border issues in Europe and elsewhere and how pissed people get when their land is invaded. "What are you doin' here?"

"She was sittin' in the dark," said Billy.

"They tell me not leave room," she said, rolling the r in room. "I not leave room."

Billy was fascinated by her voice, smooth and husky like Kathleen Turner in *Body Heat*.

Zim asked. "Who? Who told you not to leave the room?"

"Mister Vanko." Pronouncing mister as meez-tar.

Zim's brow furrowed, lips puckering, deep in thought. He dropped his forehead, eyeing her, letting her know he was about to ask a serious question and expected a serious answer. "Do you want to leave the room?"

"Of course." More than a trace of attitude.

"Ah . . . then . . . why don't you just leave the room?"

"I cannot."

"Why not?"

"Cannot disobey Mister Vanko. Is not good to disobey

ıster Vanko. Bad things happen to people who disobey Mister Vanko. You understand?"

Billy was staring at Zim, seeking guidance.

Zim asked the woman, "He your boss?"

She gave a half-laugh, cold, at the absurdity of the question. "Boss? Yes, he is boss."

Billy couldn't help himself. "And he told you to stay in this room until he came back? You shittin' me? And you're doin' it?"

Her eyes went to him. "Not smart to disobey Mister Vanko."

"So you stay in this room whenever he tells you?"

"Yes."

"That don't make sense."

She didn't respond.

Zim asked, "You related to them?"

Her mouth opened, amused. "Related?" A half-laugh. "Like sister? (seez-tar)" Another half-laugh. "No, not related."

"So what's the deal? Nobody stays in a room all day just 'cause some butthead tells 'em to."

"Mister Vanko says stay in room, I stay in room. Not smart to make Mister Vanko angry."

Billy said, "Well, you don't have to worry about that anymore." He caught a glance from Zim and his face drooped. "Shit. Sorry."

"No problem," said Zim, smoothing it over, taking it in stride. But it was a problem.

"Why?" asked the woman.

The cat was already out of the bag, thought Billy, no harm in sayin' it. "Old man Vanko's dead."

She stared at him. Then with that sultry voice cautiously asked, "What about old woman?"

Billy gave a slow nod.

Illiana smiled. It was a cold smile. "That is good. You are one who do?"

Taking pride in his craft, Billy responded, "Yeah, I did it." Wasn't often you got to talk about it, except to cons, and they were hard to impress.

The woman rose from the bed, straightened the folds on her short dress and then walked over to him, slowly, one smooth leg in front of the other, sexy. She came close, wrapping her arms around him and kissing him on the mouth, lips pressing. Billy liked it a lot but worried about first impressions—he'd had double onions on his burger in Manistique. When she was done, she took a step back. "Now we are all dead." She smiled again, this time warm, radiant, carefree. "Let's eat. You hungry? I am hungry. Not eat since yesterday. You like omelet? I am hungry for omelet."

"Guess I could use an omelet," said Billy. "What about you, Zim? You want an omelet?'

Zim shrugged. They'd just eaten an hour ago. Enough oil in the fries to grease a tractor-trailer still clinging like rancid paste to the inside of his mouth. "Yeah, sure. Why not? They got any booze?"

"Yes," she replied. "Lots of booze. I show. First, one question. You piss on face?"

It took them a moment to figure out what she was talking about, then both Billy and Zim shook their head no.

Billy said, "Didn't cross my mind."

"Mine either," said Zim.

"Plus, I got shy kidneys," said Billy then he wondered why he said it. Didn't seem manly. But it was like because she was strangely sexy he couldn't help himself and had to tell the truth, his darkest secret, pecker muscle too tight to pee after cappin' someone. He felt a wave of shame and then determined to relax and do better in the future. Feeling good after working it out, he smiled. She smiled back. Zim smiled too.

"Should have pissed on face," said Illiana. She shrugged. "Oh well, I make you omelet anyway." Then she marched past them toward the kitchen, along the way pulling a piece of tape from the door that Vanko had applied to verify obedience.

Zim and Billy agreed she was a good cook, chattering away in her hard-edged native tongue as she worked, and they were both amazed at her ability to pack away the chow. Later, stomachs distended, lounging in comfortable chairs and sipping expensive cognac in what Illiana told them was the library (although, books and all, if pushed they might have guessed), the three were strangely at ease.

"Should have pissed on face," said Illiana, picking up where she'd left off before dinner.

"What's with this pissing on the face thing you got?" asked Zim.

"Killing not enough."

Billy liked her spunk.

"What you do with bodies? Acid bath? Burn in car? Grind up and feed to pigs?"

"Nah," replied Zim. "Just dragged 'em in the bushes. They'll rot away in a year or two."

Illiana's eyes grew wide. "Drag in bushes? . . . Drag in bushes? . . . Drag in bushes not enough!" She saw the puzzled look on Billy's face and added, "Two reasons. Number one, both evil. Must crush spirit as well as kill body. Number two, Vanko connected. Body found. Evidence found. Mob find out. Then you found. Very bad."

"Now, how they gonna do that?" questioned Zim. "We were careful."

"Hah! Careful. You not watch CSI? Cops find. Mob find out. Then bad for you. Bad for me too."

After giving it some thought, the men concluded she might have a point. Billy because of the evil angle and Zim because of the mob.

"Maybe we'd better get out of here," said Billy.

Illiana shrugged. "Not necessary. No one come. Months go by, no visitors. Safe here . . . for now."

Zim cocked his head, mouth forming an o. "No one comes here?"

"No. Just gardener. He mind own business. Not come in house."

He smiled. "Cool!"

"Yes, cool. Got time to do right. Go back. Grind up Vanko and bitch. Small pieces. Feed to pigs. Maybe feel sorry for pigs."

Billy laughed. He liked her.

Zim was less impressed. "Go back? That's nuts."

She shook her head. "Not nuts. Smart. Take chainsaw. Do right. If no pigs, bury in ground, cover with lye. If not do, cops will find, mob will know, then we all dead. Slow. Not nice. Understand?"

Zim did understand. He just didn't like it. Going back to the scene of the crime was a no-no. Only stupid people did that. It was usually the last thing they did before they got caught.

Illiana said, "You not want, then I do. How long to bodies?"

"'Bout an hour and a half."

She was quiet for a moment. "Too late now, go tomorrow. Take saw. Take gas. You too squeamish, I do. You sit in car like woman."

Billy was grinning. She couldn't weigh more than a hundred pounds, tiny knockers making up only one or two. He couldn't imagine her wielding a chainsaw. Probably couldn't even lift one. Anyway, wouldn't be right. Cuttin' up bodies was man's work.

It had been a strange night indeed, thought Zim, woozy with booze and high on reefer they'd scored in Gaylord, sitting there in the library drinking 'bout the best hooch had ever passed his lips and yakkin' it up with the skinny Rusky girl-woman with the bad attitude. He was simultaneously fascinated and repulsed by her illogic. Go back to the scene of the crime? Dip people in acid? Fucking nuts! It was obvious Billy thought she was a cross between some exotic European flower and a female Charles Manson, just his type. And he was hanging on her every word. All night. Jesus! Zim couldn't wait to pass out. And maybe while he was sleeping she'd push Billy too far and he'd kill her. Now *that* would solve all their problems. Toss the house, load the Caddy, and motor west to beautiful Bemidji. With mosquito season mostly over, there'd be good times outdoors. Fishing and partying. Mainly partying. Zzzzzzz.

"Zim, wake up. We're almost there."

"Wha . . . ?"

"Zimmy, wake up, man. We're just about at the place."

Opening his bleary eyes, the first thing Zim noticed was they were moving. He was lying in the back seat of the Caddy, pillow under his head, blanket over his body, sun streaming through the windows. Why? Oh. Billy probably wanted to get on the road early. Get to Bemidji at a decent hour."

"Zim, time to work, dude. It's just up ahead. Won't take long. An hour maybe. Illiana's right, we need to crush their spirits."

"Crush spirits?" Zim had to pee and could only process one thought at a time. Glancing out a window, he noticed they were on a rural two-lane with trees on both sides. "Pull over, I gotta take a leak."

"There it is," said Billy, excited. "That's where we stopped." A moment later he slid the Caddy into the exact tire tracks left from the first time.

Zim sat up, blanket sliding to the floor. "Where are we?"

Billy turned around grinning. "Where we did the Vankos."

Zim's mouth fell open.

"Remember? We talked about it last night. We got an early start and here we are. You slept all the way." Turning to Illiana, "Well, babe, work to do. Best get started. Pop the trunk and I'll get the saw."

Illiana opened the glove box and pushed the trunk button. She smiled. "Is going to be good, Billy, very good."

Adrenaline surged through Zim's system. "Jesus Christ! Are you two insane?" His head swiveled wildly, conducting a fact check to make sure he wasn't hallucinating.

Billy was already behind the car. His muscles rippled as he hefted the saw out of the trunk. Made him feel good. Maybe strip off his shirt once he got started, show off a little, let Illiana see what he's made of. Illiana left Zim stuttering in the back seat and joined Billy, the two strolling away like lovers on a picnic, chainsaw between them, into the brushy woods.

Zim was outside next to the car relieving himself when he heard the first sputtering yank on the starter cord. On the second pull, the saw came to life. "Please, please, please let this be a dream," he muttered, flapping his dick around to get the last drops off. It was still in his hand as the State Police cruiser pulled up behind the Caddy, noise of its arrival masked by the saw. "Oh, fuck me!" said Zim when he saw the cop, tucking his unit back in his pants but forgetting to do the zipper, the saw screaming like an injured rhino not forty feet away as Billy gunned it to power through some tough hip bone.

The officer stared at him through the windshield of the cruiser. A beefy man with a large head, mid-fifties, seen it all. Zim forced a smile, showing off a missing bicuspid. The cop was on the radio. "Shit, shit, shit!" said

Zim, his mouth frozen in a ventriloquist's grin. The cop was getting out of the car now. Adjusting his belt. Hand on his gun. The gun! Where was the Glock? Zim prayed it wasn't lying on the front seat. And the saw kept up its incessant roar. RrrrrrrrrrRrrrrrrrrrRrrrRrrrrrr. The cop walked to about ten feet from Zim, stopped. "What's going on?"

Zim was at a complete loss. "Ah . . . ah. . . . ah."

Just then, Illiana strode out of the woods. Seeing the cop, she walked directly to him. "What is problem?"

The officer looked down at her, struggling to absorb the weird confluence of a skinny Rusky woman, the Caddy, Zim (wiry brown hair shooting out, flannel shirt askew, zipper open, proudly waving a flag of black underwear dotted with green frogs) plus the sound of the saw. Rrrrrrrrrrrrrr.

"I ask, what is problem?" repeated Illiana, a note of irritation in her voice.

"Doing some wood cutting?" queried the cop.

"Yes. Go camping. Need wood for fire."

The cop eyed her. "Got some blood on your shirt." Taking a half step back. "You wanna tell me about it?"

She glanced down, noticed the splatter. "Friend get splinter. I pull out. Squirt blood." She said it matter-of-factly, poking at the stain on her breast, making a small tit wiggle under her thin blue T-shirt. Closing the subject with, "I fix. He okay now." RrrrrrrRrrrrr, Billy was working on the legs.

"Gotta be careful with those saws," said the cop.

"Yes," said Illiana. "Is easy to cut flesh and bone. Can be dangerous."

"Whatcha got in the trunk?" he asked.

Zim was in panic mode. Illiana stayed cool. "Gas for saw."

"Let's have a look." Using a finger to lift the half-closed lid, he cautiously peered inside. The gas can was nestled between two round-point shovels and a large bag of lye. "Kind of dangerous keeping gas in the trunk. And the cap's leaking."

Zim noted it was, a thin sheen of liquid glistening on the top of the can and a few drops dribbling down the side. Sharp smell of petroleum in the air.

The cop said, "Gotta be careful with that stuff."

"Is okay," argued Illiana. "Shovels and bag hold up."

"I tend to disagree, little lady. The can's too full and the cap doesn't seal. If that bag moves, it'll tip. Could be a nasty fire."

"No worry. I fix."

Just then the saw died and Billy yelled from the woods, "Outta gas, hon. Bring the can."

Illiana smiled at the cop. "Must bring gas to boy-friend." She grabbed the can and turned away, striding into the woods until out of sight.

"She's a pistol," quipped Zim, immediately in anguish over his choice of words.

The cop stared at the two shovels and bag. DANGER! LYE! HARMFUL TO SKIN! "What's that stuff for?"

Zim went blank. The jig was up. "Shit."

"That's good," replied the cop. "It's important to dispose of human waste properly."

"Yes, important," said Illiana, walking back toward them. "Human waste cannot be left on ground to rot.

Must bury. Put lye on top, then no problem."

The cop smiled. He liked her. "I wish everyone were as ecologically conscious as you are, young lady."

"Would be good," she said. Billy had the saw going again. RrrrrrrRrrrrrRrrRrrrrrr. The cop's eyes went to the woods. "You want see woodcutting?" she asked.

Zim couldn't breathe. "No, no, no!" he croaked. "I'm sure the officer has more important things to do."

"What kind of saw you got?" asked the cop, relaxing a little.

"Is Homelite XL-16," was her cheerful reply. "You want see? I can show."

A sharp pain shot through Zim's chest. He clutched the car for stability.

"Nah, got one myself. Good all-around saw. Gotta keep that chain lubed though or it'll heat up and stretch, fly right off the bar."

"Saw need oil? Did not know. Thought just gas. Where put in?"

"The cap on the side is for the chain oil."

"Good to know."

"Got any oil?"

"No, but not have much more to cut."

The cop smiled. "Better safe than sorry. There's a half quart in the trunk of the cruiser. Let me get it for you."

As the trooper was fetching the oil, Zim heard the saw stop and only seconds later spied Billy peering at him through the trees like a puckish elf, spots of blood and bits of human meat sticking to his face. Zim made a shooing motion with his hand, demanding, no, *begging* Billy to stay in the woods. Billy was laughing at him.

Zim could hear it.

The cop came back around the cruiser with a half used plastic bottle of Pennzoil 10-40. "This should get you through."

"You nice man," said Illiana, giving him a warm smile.

"All part of the job," he replied. The radio crackled, followed by a stream of gibberish. The officer's brow furrowed. His hand slid down to his holster. Zim was about to run. "Well, nice talkin' to you folks. Enjoy your camping trip." Then he climbed into his cruiser, executed a three-point turn, flipped on his lights, and sped away.

"Need bag of lye," said Illiana to Zim as she grabbed the shovels. "Not much time. Must work fast."

# Four

**B**ack at Vanko's castle after burial detail, Zim was in a daze. He'd done some crime in his forty years, plenty of it, but never, ever cutting up bodies with a power saw then sluicing the gory goop into a pit and hearing the sloppy thuk of rocks hitting the bloody mound of meat-jelly as the hole was filled. It was over the line. It was *way* over the line. Completely alien to his senses. Billy and Illy (as Zim had caustically begun calling her) were in the kitchen giggling like girls at a pajama party. Zim didn't want any part of it and had wandered into the media room, leather easy chairs, moody lighting, massive flat screen, a small movie theater. He was staring at the blank screen trying to decide if he wanted to watch TV or just get drunk. He already had a bottle in his hand, so maybe the decision had been made.

Zim Crenshaw thought of himself as an optimist, but try as he might, he couldn't envision this thing turning out well. Doing the deputy was bad enough, but necessary.

Then the Vankos, well, had to. But the mob angle was disturbing. Very disturbing. And not just the mob, the Russian mob. Jesus! Wrong people to mess with. Once they found out, they'd never stop looking. And they'd sure as hell get him if he ever landed back in the joint. So, as much as he hated to admit it, Illiana was right about getting rid of the bodies. But now they were back at Vanko's house. Good lord! Why? What if a carload of his mob pals drop by? It wouldn't take them a second to see through our bullshit. Then things would turn ugly. Real ugly.

Billy popped the top off a Heineken liberated from a fridge the size of a tool shed then gazed around the large, exquisitely appointed French kitchen: high ceiling, amber woodwork, warm lighting, rich hardwood floor. The south-facing wall had an array of windows to bring in the sunlight and a pair of French doors leading to an inviting patio. Billy opened one of the doors and stepped out onto a thirty-foot semicircle of granite enclosed by stone balusters and a cap rail wide enough to dance on. Gazing beyond it, he saw an extravagant English garden where a half acre had been sculpted into an intricate work of living art. Bordered by forest, a flagstone path wound its way through ornamental trees, manicured grass, boulders green with moss, mounds of heather and row upon row of lilacs, hibiscus, geraniums, trilliums, roses, sunflowers, zinnias, marigolds, lupines and more, each group identified by a nameplate on a metal holder. Near the center was a tall fountain, and the relaxing sound of falling water filled the air.

Billy strolled across the patio and set his beer on the

rail. Waves of color vied for his attention. He'd never seen anything like it. Odd, he thought. He'd been in the castle less than twenty-four hours, a mob guy's castle, a mob guy he'd just buried in the woods and whose pals would fillet him into chum if they ever found out, yet he felt comfortable and at ease. He'd never been in a house this grand. Not even close. Strictly speaking, he'd never lived in a house, sometimes an apartment, usually a trailer, usually a crappy one at that. They always smelled of sweat and grease and booze and other odors that Billy didn't want to think about. And they were never clean, not before, during, or after his stay. And they were always small. This place, this castle, was huge and beautiful and clean, and there were loads of groceries in the pantry and gallons of liquor and soft beds and Illiana too. And everything combined made Billy want to freeze this moment in time so he could stay in it, living the dream, not forever, because even he knew that was impossible, but at least for a while.

Illiana was next to him. She placed her hand on his and whispered to him, "Is time for sex." Then she led him upstairs.

Zim had been drinking for over two hours and was zoning in the media room, staring at the blank screen as though enraptured, a Technicolor movie of his life playing in his head. At the *rap, rap, rap* of the doorknocker, he nearly soiled himself. *The mob is here!* Christ almighty, his worst nightmare! Billy has the Glock. Where is he? Then Zim heard two pairs of feet tippy-tapping on the hardwood flooring coupled with the childish prattle of Illy and Billy as they troddled to the door. He knew it was going to be a disaster. Whether mob or cops, there'd be gunfire. Then more cops and more gunfire, and sometime during the melee he would be shot dead. They'd report the number of bullet holes as dozens. He heard the heavy front door creak open and a man's voice, strangely quiet and respectful. Then Illiana talking. Him talking again, then Illiana, then the sound of the door closing. No mob, no cops, no shooting. Zim relaxed. Maybe just the gardener.

After the richness of the previous evening's cognac, Zim had opted for Jack Daniels neat. The bottle next to him was a third empty. He was taking a long sip as Billy and Illy strode into the room.

"Hey man," said an ebullient Billy. "Looks like we got us some work."

"Huh?"

"Yeah, bro. Dude came to the door wants to see Vanko 'bout whackin' someone."

Zim's face contorted in disbelief.

"He was all weepy and sayin' please and he was sorry if he'd made a mistake and shit like that."

"Grovel like dog," said Illiana.

Billy chuckled. "Illiana told him it'd be twenty grand and he got all smiley."

A muscle in Zim's neck began to spasm. He pounded on it with a fist to make it stop.

Billy continued, "Said the money wasn't a problem but he wanted to talk to Vanko in person. Illiana asked if he'd ever met him. He said no, just knew him by reputation." Billy grinned. "Zim, man, this is perfect!"

"Perfect?" replied Zim, his face in a petrified grimace.

"Yeah man, think! *Road money!"*

The road? Yes, of course, get on the road. Get the hell out of here before something terrible happens. His expression returned to an approximation of normal. "Road money," he mumbled. "But how we gonna get it without him meeting Vanko?"

"That's the beautiful part," said Billy. He eyed Illiana. "Tell him."

Hands on her hips as if having to explain something that would be obvious to a child. "He want killing done, right?"

"Right," said Zim.

"He not know Vanko, right?"

"Right"

"He know I not Vanko."

"I hope so."

"Billy too young to be Vanko."

Zim's shoulders sagged. He knew where this was leading. "I am *not* impersonating a known mobster! Jesus! Do you have an idea of what they'd do to me if they found out? No. No way."

"They not find out. Who tell? Not you. Not me. Not Billy. Not mister no-guts who pay us. Don't worry. You can be Vanko. Will be easy. Lots of clothes upstairs. I make fit. You look good. Make look rich and mean. I call number. You sit in room behind desk like in *Godfather*. Dim light. Use makeup make seem older. Man come. You tell twenty thousand. Ten before, ten after. Good money for easy work."

"I'm not doin' it."

The next day.

Vanko's office was a perfect setting, dark pecan paneling, dark patterned carpet, moody paintings, drab books in a large case against one wall, and a depressing collection of weaponry displayed on the others: rifles, pistols, a blunderbuss, two submachine guns, a variety of swords and knives, a sickle, a spear, battle axe, cudgel, mace, ebony nunchucks, various brass knuckles, and a tomahawk with a dark stain on the blade. At the far end of the room, in front of curtained windows, was a large Victorian desk with a high-backed leather chair. Zim stood next to the chair wearing a coal-black Luigi Borelli suit that, with four hours of Illiana's needlework invested, actually seemed to fit. Underneath was a black high-count cotton shirt, open at the collar, with a white silk ascot flowing from it. She rounded out his ensemble with diamond cufflinks, a Rolex Yachtmaster, and a pair of black Tanino Crisci shoes with white button-up spats. When Zim balked at the spats, she insisted they were Vanko's trademark and he had to wear them. Zim thought they made him look like a fey pimp destined to get his ass kicked.

The office curtains were drawn tight, the lighting moody, Zim's face in the shadow. There was an accent highlighting the diamonds and a subtle spot illuminating the place where the mark would sit. He was on his way.

Illiana dressed in her maid's garb for the meeting and squeezed Billy into one of Vanko's Armani suits that, owing to his rough hands, was like a flashing sign announcing 'I am a high-priced thug.' She told him not to speak and to look tough. An easy assignment. He was delighted she understood his strengths.

Standing next to Zim at the desk, she gave him his final instructions. "Don't talk much. Get name, get address, get description, get money. Tell bring other half one day after hit. Tell bad things happen if not bring money. Then say not worry, you handle, you take care of problem."

"Easy money," said Billy. "Road money."

"Yes, road money," said Illiana. "Must leave country. Argentina maybe."

"Argentina?"

"Not go, cops will find. They not forget about deputy."

Zim glared at Billy. "You told her about the deputy?"

Billy shrugged. "Why not?"

Before Zim could formulate a response, there was a rapping at the door. "Sit," said Illiana. Zim sat. Reaching into her pocket, she removed two balls of fluff. Holding them out, "You want cotton for cheeks like Brando?"

Zim's brow wrinkled. "What?"

"Not important." She stuffed them back in her crisply pressed dress. "Just try look mean."

Zim put on his hardest jailhouse face.

Illiana sighed. "Do best you can. Get money. Billy and I handle rest."

Round and soft with small features and an ingratiating manner that Illiana sensed would easily turn to cruelty if he ever had the upper hand, she led the mark into Vanko's office and pointed to a chair in front of the desk where Zim sat like a scowling, hawk-nosed sphinx.

Fingers worrying the brow of his plaid trilby, the mark said, "Mr. Vanko, thank you for seeing me."

Zim gave a slow nod and then reached deep for the

breathy voice gang bosses have in the movies. He gestured to the chair. "Take a seat, mister . . ."

"No names please."

Zim glared at him. Added a rasp. "You come to my house. You ask for me by name. You want me to do things for you, dangerous things. But you, you want to be safe, anonymous, as though I'm not going to find out who you are."

The mark winced.

"So tell me now, who is asking me to whack someone. Then we talk price. Then it happens. Understand?"

The mark gave a quick, obedient nod. "Yes, yes, of course. My name is Kettleman, Charles Kettleman. And the person I want dead is my wife."

How original, thought Zim. "Yeah, fine. Standard scale, twenty for the job. Ten now, ten after."

His lips pinched. "Twenty's a little steep. Couldn't you come down a bit?"

"No can do, but I'll give you half off on a second."

Kettleman appeared shocked. "Good god, man! What do you think I am, a monster?"

Zim smiled and raised a hand, waving the thought away like Vito Corleone. "Relax, Mr. Kettleman, it's a joke."

Kettleman forced a weak grin.

"So, we good to go or what?" asked Zim. "I ain't got all day."

"Yes, yes! Fine. When can you do it?"

"Hmm . . ." Vanko's leather-bound daytimer was on the desk. Zim pretended to consult it. "Today's Tuesday . . . um . . this week's pretty jammed up. Got a hit in

Milwaukee on Wednesday, some leg-breaking in Duluth Thursday." He flipped a page. "Looks like we have an opening on Friday." He eyed Kettleman, whose mouth was agape, and waited for his response.

"Friday's fine. I'll make sure I'm out of town on business. A perfect alibi." He paused, lips twitching, then leaned forward and whispered. "How are you going to do it?"

Zim leaned forward too, mocking him. "How would you like us to do it?"

Kettleman's mouth formed a cruel smile. "Strangulation."

Jesus! This guy's a real freak, thought Zim, but he kept his face a mask. "Kettleman, my men are professionals and they like to stay detached. Know what I mean? When it's a slug to the back of the head, it don't matter who's dying, because you're not stoppin' to get to know 'em. But when you stare into someone's eyes while you're choking the last breath out of them, well, that's something altogether different. That takes a specialist."

"I thought murder was generic."

"Actually, no, it's very specialized. But you're lucky, Kettleman, because I have the top strangler in the Midwest on my payroll. But he's not cheap. Something face-to-face like that would add to the cost. It's not for me, you understand, it's for . . . *the Squid!*"

"The Squid? That's his nickname?" Kettleman frowned. "I thought it'd be like Johnny Nails or Joey Bag o' Donuts. Something that sounded tough."

"What? You don't think a squid is tough?" Zim was amazed at Kettleman's ignorance of marine life.

Kettleman scrunched his face. "It's a blob of jelly that squirts ink out its butt."

"You're missing the point, Kettleman. It has tentacles. Get it? Tentacles? Strangulation?" Zim poked at his head with a finger. "Are you making the connection?"

Kettleman shrugged. "Not really."

Sighing in exasperation, Zim thrust his arms forward and began choking an imaginary victim. "The Squid's arms and hands are like tentacles, see? They wrap around the victim's throat and squeeze, squeeze, squeeze until the last breath is gone, the last heartbeat a memory."

"Yeah, well, I suppose. Does he go by anything else?"

"Yeah, his real name. If I tell you, you won't tell anyone else, will you? Because that would make the Squid very angry."

"No, no! Of course not!" Kettleman shifted nervously. "I absolutely do not want to know his real name."

Zim smiled. "It's five grand more for the Squid. You're sure a bullet in the brain wouldn't do just as well?"

"Um . . . the strangulation is important to me." Kettleman's eyes wandered as he did the math. "You're sure he won't come down a bit?"

Spreading his hands, Zim said, "You wanna negotiate with the Squid? Be my guest." His head tilted forward. "But I gotta warn you, he's easily offended."

Kettleman's eyes grew wide with realization. "Ah, maybe not."

Zim gave him a wink and a nod. "That seems wise."

"Twenty-five thousand. You're sure?"

"Look, Kettleman, you can go down to Detroit and find someone to do it for a pack of cigarettes. Only problem is, he'll get caught and then he'll rat you out. With us, you have insurance. We're professionals. That means we do murder right. The minute I have your deposit, your wife is as good as dead. Guaranteed. And we don't get caught. But, if it ever were to happen, nobody in my organization would talk. It's severely frowned upon. Plus, it would make matters more complicated. You see, our guys have a benefit package that includes fancy lawyers in the event of a problem. Then our man and the lawyers develop a plausible explanation as to why he drove four hundred miles from Chicago to Loon Haven, broke into a home, and was caught with his hands around the throat of a woman he had no connection to, like maybe testing a new chiropractic technique or something, and that's the only story ever told, and any witnesses either change their tune or disappear. Then the lawyers plead it down to a misdemeanor and we chalk it up to occupational hazard. And most importantly, *your* name is never mentioned. Ever. That's what the extra twenty-four thousand nine hundred ninety-five dollars is buying you."

Kettleman was convinced and told Zim he'd have the down payment to him by the next day. Zim got the details about Mrs. Kettleman, jotting them down in Vanko's day-timer like directions to the dentist. The process got him thinking about dental care and how if he ever had enough money he'd get a new tooth to fill the unsightly gap left by the missing bicuspid. The prison dentist who pulled it was a damn sadist. Didn't give him enough Novocain to dull a mosquito bite. Hurt just thinking about it. Then he realized he'd zoned off. Kettleman was staring at him.

"Just visualizing," said Zim. "I like to visualize the job."

"You do?" said Kettleman, face registering disgust.

"I love my work, Kettleman. That's why I'm at the top."

"I guess that makes sense."

# Five

"**B**illy the Squid?" said Illiana, puzzled. "What mean Billy the Squid?"

Zim was beside himself with mirth after coming up with the catchy moniker while telling Billy and Illy about Kettleman's extra payment for a strangling.

Billy grimaced. "I'm more comfortable with shooting.

Illiana said, "First time always most difficult when learn new skills."

Billy nodded.

Zim's eyes narrowed in disbelief.

"Is feeling of accomplishment when job done," she added.

Billy had never thought of killing as an accomplishment, but maybe it was.

"We go together. Do together. Will be good, Billy, very good." She gave him her warmest smile and squeezed his arm, and Billy knew with a certainty that it would be good, very good.

Kettleman brought the money as promised, and the next two days passed nervously for Zim. He'd never been part of anything close to a murder for hire scheme and couldn't shake the feeling it was a bad career move. Not that he wasn't up to his neck in murky water already, but Judas Priest, wasn't there some limit to the amount of risk a man should take? He'd tried to talk Billy and Illy into taking the twelve-five and hitting the road to Bemidji, but neither would have any part of it. And in a way they were right. They'd probably net ten fencing stuff stripped from the castle. That, along with the full twenty-five from Kettleman, would set them up for nearly a year in South America. And though he'd actually never worked, Zim felt the need for a *real* vacation, one where he didn't have to think about money or cops or the mob. South America seemed like the right place.

Billy drained his coffee cup and set it in the sink and then glanced at his glittering Rolex President, a gift from Illiana. She knew where the good stuff was. "I guess it'll take about an hour."

"Is eight-thirty now," said Illiana to Zim. "There will be no problem, but always good to plan. We not back by midnight means cops have. Call lawyer. Use Kettleman money pay bail. Understand? Just like story you tell Kettleman. After get out, we blackmail for more money then leave town."

"Right," answered Zim. It wasn't a half-bad plan. His plan really, but it was coming out of her mouth. She was telling him to use his own plan. Life is weird.

Billy and Illy had cased the Kettleman house the day
before, 325 Sturgeon Lane, a small, drab ranch-style in
a neighborhood of small, drab ranch-styles. Now they
cruised past, turned around, parked. Streetlights on the
block, but none in front of the house. A boy ran toward
them on the sidewalk, dashed across a yard, disappeared.
The street was deserted. "Is time," said Illiana. Billy
nodded.

No one saw them as they strolled to the Kettleman
residence and up to the door. Illy rang the bell, the latex
glove on her hand making the button feel squishy. The
porch light went on, and the door opened. Illiana smiled
at the woman framed in the warm glow from the inside.
The woman smiled back, the aroma of freshly baked
cookies wafting into the cool night air.

"Car break. Can use phone?"

"Your car broke?" said the woman, her kind face displaying concern. "Why, of course, dear. Come on in."

"Something smell good."

"I just took some cookies out of the oven. Would you
like one?"

Billy was flexing his fingers. Billy the Squid.

It was only nearing ten. Zim was pacing the floor in
the kitchen of the castle, hand strangling the neck of a
Blue Ribbon, wondering if maybe he should be loading
up one of Vanko's other cars, just in case. There was a
black Range Rover in the garage. That would do. If they
weren't back by midnight, no doubt about it, he had to
go. Yes, he'd contact a bail bondsman and a lawyer, but

he'd do it from another state. Jesus, a contract killing! He'd always imagined himself a dashing outlaw riding the dusty fringes of legal society, sometimes in, sometimes out. But this wasn't the fringe anymore, this was serious shit, and he was in it up to his eyeballs, and South America was looking more and more attractive to him every minute. One of those countries where the Nazis went with no extradition, or at least none if you knew who to grease. He already knew a few curse words in Spanish. They weren't so hard. He could probably pick up the lingo quick. And with American dollars being *mucho gusto*, he could be a big gringo around town, dressin' sharp and trolling for ladies, driving something that wouldn't break down every goddamned day like his last piece of crap Kia. Twenty-five grand plus whatever they could plunder from the castle adding another ten or even twenty to it, yeah, forty-five grand would be hefty *dinero* down in taco land. Zim glanced at the clock, nearly a minute had gone by. "Shit, shit, shit," he mumbled. He'd just begun mentally inventorying what he should load for his getaway when he heard the front door open and the disturbingly cheery voices of the homicide twins. They ambled into the kitchen, Billy clutching a large Ziploc bag filled with chocolate chip cookies.

Holding the bag out. "Zim, you gotta try one of these. They're great!"

"Cookies?"

"Yeah, man. Try one."

"Sure. How'd it go?" Zim pulled a cookie out of the bag and took a bite. Billy and Illy watched carefully.

"Well?" asked Billy

"It's good," said Zim, eyebrows rising in affirmation. He popped the rest in his mouth and spoke while he chewed. "Where'd you get 'em?"

"Mrs. Kettleman."

Zim's throat constricted. He coughed, and a glob of semi-masticated cookie dough shot across the room and stuck on the refrigerator. Illiana made a sour face. Billy laughed. "She was taking them out of the oven when we got there. They're still warm."

"You took her cookies?"

"Why not? They would have dried out if we'd left them."

Illiana said, "Is special flavor. Maybe almond extract."

"And a hint of cinnamon," added Billy.

"I guess," said Zim whose line of logic had petered out, but something about it just wasn't right. "Did you do it?"

"Of course," replied Illy. "Was easy. Cookies are bonus. Plus, I get recipe."

"That's wonderful. Let's start loading."

Illiana said, "Should not be in hurry to leave. Two reasons. First, when Kettleman come pay, he get suspicious if see things missing. Second, next few days cops watch every car on road. Not want stand out with carload of stuff. Better to stay, not be seen."

Billy nodded agreement.

"Stay here?" Zim was incredulous. "No, no, no." He thrust out his arm and pointed in a random direction. "We gotta get across the state line to get the heat off."

Illy shook her head. "Heat on in public. Heat off if here."

The murder was the lead story on news radio during breakfast the next morning. Irma Zumwalt, 63, a widow living alone, was brutally strangled, apparently for a tray of freshly baked cookies. The Cookie Strangler, as the perpetrator had been dubbed, took only the cookies and the recipe for them, which had been ripped from her notebook. "A shocking and heinous crime that cries out for justice," said Loon Haven police chief Chan Rooney in an interview. "Mrs. Zumwalt was the nicest person in town. Everyone loved her. And her prize-winning cookies were the best. It's as though there was a hint of almond and cinnamon in each bite. Our entire department is on the case and won't rest until the perpetrator is behind bars."

When Zim heard the name, his muscles went slack. "What? What was that name? Zumwalt?" He stared at Illy and then Billy. They stared at each other. "You killed the wrong woman!"

"Could not be," said Illy. "Was address Kettleman gave. Woman fit description." She became thoughtful. "Maybe Kettleman lie, say want wife killed but really want other."

"But why?"

"Not know. Love triangle, blackmail, cookie grudge, does not matter. Only matter Kettleman pay rest of money. Then maybe slap to get truth."

They waited all day and well into the evening before Kettleman showed, Zim chafing in his godfather duds, Billy and Illy alternating between eating, giggling, and noisy sex in one of the castle's many rooms. Zim assumed they were trying to work their way through the entire house. He estimated they were well on their way to doing it. At 10:30 they heard a rapping. Zim dashed into the office, Illy went to the door, Billy stayed out of sight. Illiana led Kettleman to Zim's office and left the two alone. Kettleman was not a happy camper.

"Your guy screwed up and did the wrong woman. I want my money back."

"What? You're the one who gave us the address, Kettleman, 325 Sturgeon Lane." Zim's finger jabbed at Vanko's daytimer. "I've got it written down right here."

"325 *North* Sturgeon Lane, not 325 *South* Sturgeon Lane. Doesn't that nimrod know how to read?"

Zim leafed through the daytimer to the page where he'd written the address. His shoulders sagged when he saw he'd only written Sturgeon Lane, not *North* Sturgeon Lane. The rest of the screw up was easy to fathom. Billy and Illy had found Sturgeon Lane and a house numbered 325 and that was it. Time for butt covering. "You didn't say *North* Sturgeon Lane, Kettleman. I wrote down the exact address you gave me and there's no north in it. It's your screw up. The job's done. The Squid wants his money."

"What! No way."

Zim gave him a hard stare. "It would be a serious mistake to shortchange the Squid."

Kettleman's lips puckered in disgust. "Well, you can tell Mr. Squid that I don't appreciate his sloppy work and I'm not paying a dime. The job wasn't done. That means I get a refund."

Zim's face opened in disbelief. He gestured to the display of killing tools adorning the room. "Does this look like Wal-Mart? There are no refunds. None, nada, put that out of your mind. But I don't want you to go away unsatisfied, the fifty-percent-off offer still stands. What say the Squid whacks the missus tonight and we all sleep like babies?"

"Another killing so soon? Wouldn't that be suspicious?"

Zim shrugged. "Just some nut on a crime spree."

"But the addresses have symmetry, 325 North and 325 South on the same street. That's going to draw attention."

"Pure coincidence. I doubt anyone will even notice."

"Geez, I don't know."

"Kettleman, don't you understand? It's better this way. The cops will think they have a random serial killer on the loose and they won't suspect you of a thing."

"I suppose."

"It's just a few more dollars, Kettleman. You're buying quality here. You're buying the perfect setup. You still want her dead, don't you?"

"Yes, of course."

"Then why wait? This is the opportunity of a lifetime, and no one will ever suspect a thing. All for only an additional twelve-five. It's the bargain of the century, a blue light special."

"Oh, all right."

"Good. How about tonight?"

"So soon?"

"Sure," said Zim, surprised at Kettleman's reticence. "When there's work to be done, no sense putting it off."

"Um . . . okay. Tell me when to be gone and I'll figure out an alibi."

"Make yourself scarce between nine and midnight. It'll be done by then."

"More work," said Zim as Billy and Illy crowded the kitchen table, anxious for news of the second payment.

"What about money," asked Illiana, Zim's demeanor telegraphing he didn't have it.

Sensing her ire, Zim became defensive. "Kettleman was pissed, but it was all his fault." He went on to describe the mix-up, changing key elements to distance himself from blame. "So, I told him we'd go half off on the wife. Another twelve-five. That means there'll be twenty-five grand due and payable after she's done."

"You not get money," said Illiana flatly.

"How could I? The dude was pissed. I had to make a deal."

"Now Billy and I must take extra risk. That not good. First time easy, no one suspicious. Now hard, everyone scared. Lucky if lone woman even answer door."

"Don't worry. It'll be easy."

"If easy, then you do," she challenged.

"What? Me? Ah, I . . ah . . . it's not really my style. I'm more of a shooter, a stabber if I have to be, but I'm not much of a choker. Know what I mean? It's a matter of preference."

"My preference get money," said Illy, sensing Zim didn't have the guts for it. "Should have made Kettleman pay."

"Told you, he was pissed. There was nothing I could do. I made the best deal I could."

Billy shrugged. "It is an extra twelve-five, hon. Maybe we should do it."

Illy and Billy straggled back into the castle near midnight, just before Zim's anxiety meter went redline. Billy was sporting a fat lip. Illy had a scratch on her arm. "How'd it go?"

"Problems," answered Billy.

"Like what?"

"Some dude was there. Had to do 'em both."

Zim pictured a never-ending line of bodies on gurneys in the morgue. "Oh."

"Was boyfriend," said Illy. "That why Kettleman want hit."

"Oh."

"Now Kettleman get real deal, wife and boyfriend too."

"I'm sure he'll be thrilled," said Zim, the bodies in his imaginary morgue sitting up and staring. Now pointing. Pointing at him.

# Six

"**What's the matter** with you people?" barked Kettleman before he'd even sat down in Zim's office. "Can't you do anything right?"

"What's the matter with *you*, Kettleman? We do you a favor and you're still not happy."

"That dumbass Squid killed my brother!"

"Well, maybe your brother shouldn't have been doin' your wife. Ever think of that?"

"He wasn't *doing* my wife, he was passing through town on business and stopped by to visit."

"Just passing through, oldest story in the book. And you believe it?"

"He lives in Hastings, Minnesota, and hasn't been here in over a year. He sells medical devices. His wife said he was on his way to Detroit for a trade show and thought he'd surprise us. He was *not* my wife's boyfriend, so get that out of your head. He was my brother. Jesus! That nitwit Squid killed my brother!"

"Shit happens," said Zim, "but what's done is done. Did you bring the money?"

"Twelve-five, but that's all," He reached into his jacket for an envelope, angrily tossing it on the desk. "And you can tell ink butt I said he's a fuck up and should consider another line of work."

Zim deliberated before responding. "Kettleman, you shouldn't fuck with the Squid. He knows where you live."

"Yeah, well considering his track record with addresses, I think I'm safe. Goodbye."

"It's a matter of principle," said Zim. "He cheated us. We have to whack him."

Kettleman was gone, and they were sitting at around the kitchen table.

"Ink butt? He really called me ink butt?" Billy's hackles were up.

"Not good," said Illiana, "but not important. Must think of big picture."

"What big picture?" asked Zim. The little picture was the big picture to him. Kettleman's neck filled the frame.

"Big picture is not get caught, go South America, live good life. That big picture. Now have twenty-five thousand. Much more in bank. Must drain accounts, stay quiet then rent truck, load valuables, sell in big city."

"How much do you think it'll add up to?" asked Billy.

Illiana shrugged. "Hard to tell. Million maybe. Vanko has more, but would be hard to get."

Billy's eyes opened wide. "A million! Wow!"

"Yes, wow. Live good life, Billy." She squeezed his arm.

Zim was in shock. A million dollars! It was almost too much. Nothing that good could ever happen to him. There must be a catch. "So, exactly how are we supposed to get the money in the bank accounts?"

"Easy," said Illy. "Do like with Kettleman."

"And how's that?"

She gave him a do-I-really-have-to-explain-this look. "Go to bank and close account."

Zim coughed a laugh. "You?"

"No."

"Billy?"

She shook her head.

Zim stepped back. "Whoa! Wait a minute. Not me. I am not going into a bank with guards and cops and bank managers itching to find something wrong and hit the panic button. That's suicide."

"I hold hand so not be nervous." Her words a cat o' nine tails of contempt, flogging him into submission.

Billy couldn't help himself and laughed.

Zim couldn't speak.

"So, it's settled," said Billy. "We get the money, load the stuff, and maybe do Kettleman on our way out of town. It'll be fun."


Zim pouted for the next three days running, drinking heavily, purposely making himself unfit for banking or any other work while Illy and Billy methodically catalogued every item in the castle worth loading and hauling away. After due consideration, Illiana thought it best if they only took as much as would fit in one 30-foot U-Haul truck, reasoning that the trucks were so common it wouldn't draw attention to them while at the same time maximizing their take.

It was during this period that Illiana thought up a new variation on Zim's persona. After checking with him, she found he'd never given Kettleman a first name. If it ever became an issue, she thought it'd be best to have Zim say he was Victor "Mad Dog" Vanko's son, Drek. Zim was simply too young to be Victor Vanko, and there might come a time when the distinction would be important. When she suggested it, he made a face.

"Drek? What kind of name is that?"

"Old-country name. Tough. Hard. Sometime may be better than using old man's name. Safer for you."

Safer appealed to Zim, but he had to put in his two cents. "Sounds like the crud in a drain."

"How about Skunk?" offered Billy.

Illiana tittered. Zim frowned.

"How about Tyrone?" Zim had known a cool cat in the joint named Tyrone. "Or Rock? I like Rock."

Illiana's lips wrinkled in disapproval. "Not good. Too friendly. Must use name to keep distance."

He rolled his eyes. "Fine. Whatever you like."

It was early evening and Zim was in the great room—varnished timbers, granite fireplace, plush furnishings, tall windows with a view of the front yard. He was sitting in the semi-darkness on a leather couch in front of a cold fireplace sucking on a Blue Ribbon, restless and longing for a relief. He knew Illiana's plan to get Victor Vanko's money was a good plan, but it wasn't *his* plan, and he was getting tired of being told what to do. And he was bored. And owing to the never-ending sexcapades of Billy and Illy, his own unmet need for female companionship was in stark and painful contrast. He had to get out of the castle, find a bar, drink, shoot the shit, and if he were far luckier than usual, find a willing woman. But he couldn't just crank up the Caddy and go because that would bring down the wrath of Illy and Billy, the sex-crazed plan-freaks. Indeed, over the past few days Zim had come to believe that doing crime with them was as bad as having a job. Maybe worse. At least with a job if you damn well felt like it, you could go out at night. And he damn well did feel like it. But he knew he'd have to have an excuse. And if he couldn't think of one, he'd have to sneak out. As Zim was pondering possible escape scenarios, he reflected on the fact that he was forty years old. His shoulders sagged. How could a life go so wrong?

Illy and Billy lay in a sweaty tangle on the huge four-poster bed of the bedroom they'd commandeered, both exhausted. It was their fourth time that day. Billy was proud of his sexual prowess and his ability to last until Illiana's huffing and bucking and squeezing told him she was there and it was his turn. Afterward, it felt so good to have her lying next to him—Illiana, beautiful and sexy and wild. And she was smart too, so he didn't have to worry about thinking, which was a big relief. Yes, it was far better than good, it was the best, and he absolutely did not want it to end. It was his image of perfection. Nothing short of a dream come true. He'd become a professional, a specialist, a contract killer, someone you could depend on to do the job right, someone worthy of respect. He was Billy the Squid, and if anyone didn't like it, he'd kill 'em. And he had a beautiful girlfriend and lived in a castle and ate the best food and drank the best booze and drove a Caddy and, except for the occasional murder, didn't have to work at all. Could life possibly be any better?

Just then, Illiana sat up, the sheet falling away. Billy stared at her tiny but perfect breasts thinking he may be ready for more feeding. "Billy, I think I make mistake."

"A mistake?"

"Yes. Maybe not need Zim go bank. He afraid, be nervous, then maybe problems."

"Yeah, ol' Zimmy's not really diggin' it. You want me to do it?"

She grinned. "Would do good, lover boy, but need not take risk. I am think we use computer to get money, make transfer, use bank card, use credit card, not let people see face so can identify later."

Billy nodded. It made sense.

"You know how use computer?" she asked.

Billy shook his head.

"Zim?"

"I doubt it."

"Me either, but we find way." She lay back down, cuddling in his strong arms. "Zim is good man, Billy, but not reliable. Must watch or he get us in trouble."

Billy nodded and began nuzzling.


An hour later, after Zim had worked up the courage, he strolled into the kitchen. Billy and Illy were still upstairs. The keys to the Caddy were lying on the counter.

He snatched them up and made for the front door. In an effort to establish plausible deniability in the event of a conflict, he whispered, "Going out for a paper. Back in a bit." Then he quietly slipped outside and slid into the Caddy.

When Illiana heard the car engine start, she jumped out of bed and hurried to a window with a view of the front yard. Gazing out, she spied the tail of the Caddy as it disappeared up the winding drive. It was Zim, of course. She knew he'd be trouble. Leaving the house was a mistake, a big mistake. Was he running off? Did he take the money? She glanced at Billy. He was asleep. Nude, she rushed downstairs to the office and checked the drawer where they'd agreed to keep their earnings. Counting it, she came up a thousand short. That meant Zim wasn't running, he was going out to party.

# Seven

**Z**im **took a** left at the highway, M-28, a two-lane winding along the southern shore of Lake Superior, determined to stop at the first bar that had girl-cars. The first place he passed had three pickups. Nope. The second, two pickups and a dozen Harleys. Not a chance. The third was a bar and restaurant called the Woodland Inn. It had dozens of cars. All kinds. Hmm. It was a little upscale, and that would be unusual for him, highly unusual, but earlier Illiana had insisted on washing his jeans and flannel shirt. Because of it, he was dressed in his Vanko duds, right down to the clean white spats, and figured he'd be a better fit at the Woodland Inn than in a biker bar. He parked the Caddy and strolled to the entrance. Pulling himself straight, he flexed his arms, rolled his shoulders, and walked in.

The bar, an oval with seats around, was straight ahead, there was a dance floor to the right with a band tuning up on a bandstand, and there were loads of women. *Jackpot!*

Zim sensed he was getting more than a few stares as he strode to the rail. Even more when he pulled out a fat roll and peeled off five twenties, sliding them across to the bartender.

"Courvoisier Cognac, neat, and keep 'em coming."

"Yes sir."

The drink was in front of him in an instant.

"May I have your name, sir?"

He almost said Zim. Then he smiled and said, "Drek. Drek Vanko." Nodding at the bills, "And take one for yourself."

The bartender peeled off a Jackson. "Thanks, Mr. Vanko. Let me know if you need anything."

"I'll do that."

As Zim turned to scan the crowd, the band broke into its first song, "Proud Mary," one of his favorites, and he began bobbing his head to the beat. He was six bobs in when the most amazing thing happened. An attractive redhead in a frilly red western shirt and skin-tight jeans walked up to him and asked him to dance. From now on I'm wearing this suit 24/7, he thought as he slid off the barstool. "Damn right, girl. Let's rip it up."

Illiana sat in the Godfather chair, bare butt on the cool leather, pondering the possible consequences of Zim's absence. In all probability, nothing would come of it. Zim would find a cheap bar, get drunk, hit on some women, be rejected by all, get drunker, and eventually make his way back to the castle. Even so, there was always the chance that he might say the wrong thing, bragging, trying to impress someone. And the last time she'd seen him, he was wearing his mobster suit. He'd stand out like a clown at a funeral. People would stare, remember, be able to identify him later from a mug shot or in a line-up. Stupid, stupid, stupid! She was berating herself, not him. She'd been having so much fun with Billy that she'd forgotten it might be difficult for Zim, him not having any companionship. She should have made inquiries and hired a professional to keep him happy. Someone from Chicago. Pay the fare. Someone who could keep her mouth shut and evaporate when the job was done. Damn! If Zim didn't screw things up tonight and force them on the run, or worse, that's the first thing she'd do in the morning. He'd thank her for it, and be much easier to handle. Nevertheless, there was still tonight to worry about.

"Billy . . . Billy." She gently stroked his arm.

"Humh?" he mumbled, coming to life.

"Billy! Must get up. Zim is gone. Must find and watch. Make sure not do wrong."

Billy blinked his eyes open. "Zim's gone?"

"Yes. Probably go to bar, look for woman."

He grinned. "Yeah, probably."

"Took thousand dollars. Dressed in Godfather suit. Am worrying he bring attention. Must find and watch. If problem, we can fix. Understand?"

Billy nodded. Other than Zim getting drunk and shooting off his mouth, he wasn't sure what kind of problem there might be. Or, if there were a problem, what he and Illiana could do about it. But Illiana seemed to know, and that was good enough for him. He sat up in bed. Illiana was sitting on the edge. He brushed his hand across the smooth skin of her thigh. He wanted to pull her down on the Egyptian cotton and forget about Zim for another hour or two, feel her luxurious hair in his fingers and her supple body against his, but he knew it wasn't going to happen. "Gimme a minute, hon. I gotta pee."

It took less than twenty minutes from the time they left the castle to find him, a lucky guess turning in the direction away from Loon Haven, the same way Zim had gone. They slowed for two watering holes, scanning the cars and searching for the Caddy before spying it in the parking lot at the third, a rustic but well-kept bar and restaurant with an extravagant view of Lake Superior. Billy parked the Range Rover and they walked arm-in-arm to the door.

Illiana said, "If Zim see, we go to him. Talk, drink, relax, make like no problem. If Zim not see, we find table in dark corner. Watch, make sure no trouble."

Billy nodded. Like Zim, Illiana could plan on the fly. But when they entered the establishment and scanned the crowd, Zim could not be seen.

"There," said Billy. "On the dance floor." He pointed toward the middle of the crowd. Sure enough, Illiana recognized Zim's slicked-back hair bouncing up and down amid a sea of bodies.

"Must find table." She gave Billy's sleeve a tug and he followed her to the most distant corner of the restaurant that still had a view of the bar and dance floor. A waitress appeared with menus. The special was all-you-can-eat fried perch. Impossible to resist. Beer to wash it down.

Zim was on his third dance, a slow one, and the redhead was wrapped around him like she meant it. He thought maybe he'd start sleeping in the suit. The dance ended. He was thirsty. "What say we sally on up to the bar and have a drink?" The redhead nodded. Zim ushered his prize to his station then raised a finger to catch the bartender's attention, but an older man rushed over first.

"Your money's no good here, Mr. Vanko." He pushed the stack of bills toward Zim.

The hair stood up on the back of Zim's neck. He was ready to go jailhouse on him out of pride. This was sure to mess up his chance with the redhead. He leaned into the bar and put on a snarly face. "You got a problem?"

The man's hands went up in a gesture of peace. "No, no, not at all. Like I said, Mr. Vanko, your money's no good here. Drinks are on the house for you and your lady friend. Dinner too, if you like. If I do say so myself, the perch fry is excellent."

"On the house?" It was a phrase Zim had never heard. It took him a while to comprehend its meaning and implications.

"Of course, sir," said the man. "Anything you like. I'm Frank Thurman, the owner." He stuck out a pudgy hand. Zim shook it.

"Oooh," cooed the redhead, squeezing Zim's arm.

The couples to their left and right were watching the exchange in awe. The woman on Zim's left, more than a little drunk, eyed him up and down then curled her lip. "What makes you so special?" Hearing it, her husband's eyes went wide. He grabbed her arm and pulled her close, urgently whispering something into her ear. Then her mouth opened and her eyes darted to Zim. "Sorry, Mr. Vanko," said the man as he dragged his startled wife off her barstool and toward the exit. "She's a little into her cups. No offense, okay? No offense."

Zim shrugged. "No harm, no foul. You two have a nice evening."

"Oooh, said the redhead, gluing herself to Zim and running a hand up his thigh, fingers brushing against his business.

The fried perch was incredibly good. Billy was packing down filet number seven. Illiana was on her fourth as she kept a sharp eye on what she could see of Zim and the redhead Velcroed to him. Out of the corner of her eye she saw a man walk in the entrance. Large. Sturdy. A scowl formed on his face. He was staring in the direction of Zim and the redhead. His demeanor soured further as he stalked toward them. Illiana went on full alert. If Zim got into a fight and the police came, they'd insist on seeing identification. She prayed he wasn't carrying any. He was wanted, for godsake! Having it on him would be suicide. Nevertheless, there was little doubt that if the cops came, Zim would end up in jail. A first-degree murder charge for the deputy in Gaylord. No death penalty in Michigan. Life without parole. Maybe second degree and an easy ten if he gave up Billy. It would only be a matter of time before he caved. There was no alternative, she and Billy had to get involved.

"Billy!" He looked up from his plate. "Trouble for Zim. Redhead have boyfriend. Boyfriend not happy. Must make sure no fight, no cops." Through with explanations, she bounded from her chair and wove through the tables toward the bar where Zim was sitting unawares. Billy was close behind. She saw the man peel the redhead off Zim and then step forward and grab him by the lapels. "Guess what?"

"What?" responded Zim deadpan. He'd been in this situation before—the awkward love triangle with the inevitable fight over the woman—and he had a three-drink confidence he could handle the peckerhead.

"Anyone messes with my girl gets their ass kicked, fuckwad."

Illiana hurried up to them and stared at the man. "You got problem?"

The man gave her a dismissive glance then turned back to Zim.

"Hey!" said Illiana. Her arm flashed up, hand slapping his face with a sharp crack. "I ask question, expect answer. One more chance. You got problem?"

His head swiveled toward her, face contorting in disbelief. "Fuck you, you skinny bi—" Billy decked him before the last word was out. The band stopped playing. Everyone's head turned. A silence descended upon the crowd.

"Not nice man," said Illiana to the staring patrons. She pointed toward the body on the floor. "Drink too much. Get mean. Now sleep. Is good, yes?" She smiled and nodded.

Laughter rippled through the crowd, and a chorus of *Yes!* was heard as the owner and the bartender dragged the unfortunate swain toward the door.

"Now is time for fun!" she said, throwing her arms in the air and nodding at the bandstand. Taking its cue, the musicians broke into "Brown Sugar" and the dancers resumed bouncing.

"I was about to handle it," said Zim, adjusting his ascot. The redhead was back at his side. She gave him a smooch on the cheek and began rubbing his back. Spoils to the victor. "What are you two doing here?"

"Perch fry," said Illiana. "Is good. You two want eat? Come join," she urged, nodding at the woman, encouraging her to say yes.

The redhead turned to Zim. "Hungry, Mr. Vanko?"

Zim blinked. He thought maybe he'd fallen into a cosmic wormhole and been transported to a different dimension, one where women actually liked him. He gave her a warm smile. "Starved."

"Is settled," said Illiana, herding them toward the table. Flagging down a waitress along the way, she ordered a drink for everyone and two for Zim. She wanted him sedated, flexible, and open to suggestion; specifically, going directly back to the castle after dinner and never showing his face outside its granite walls again until the U-Haul was packed and ready to roll. But she knew with a woman's certainty that Zim was locked and loaded and would insist on ushering the redhead home for target practice. She doubted anything other than passing out could dissuade him. So, that, of course, was her number one goal as she ordered round after round for him. Second to that would be to minimize the damage.

Although lubricated to a frictionless state previously achieved only in cryogenic experiments costing millions, Zim would not pass out, the sex drive being too strong and him being without for a very long time. And, to his unbridled delight, the redhead, who said her name was Remy Torriano, was giving every indication she was willing, perhaps sensing Drek Vanko was too interesting to pass up. Illiana resigned herself to plan B, minimizing the damage that would occur when Zim brought the woman back to the castle for bed fun. She was sure to have friends. She would tell them. They would tell others. Everyone would know. She and Billy needed to construct a portrait of Drek Vanko that was soft and appealing, something to win confidence and friends, not inquiries and enemies. She bided her time until the moment was right and then said to Remy, "Drek good man. You get to know, you like. Not mean like gangster father."

"Oooh," replied the redhead. She gazed at Zim as if he were a god, fingers smoothing the front of his suit coat.

With plan B pretty much in place, Illiana had only to be sociable at dinner, and later, a congenial host at the castle without revealing anything of a worrisome nature. That night it was Zim's turn to be playful and Billy and Illy's to be nervous. When morning came and Zim and the redhead didn't make an early appearance, she became even more worried. They finally fell out of the sack about ten and stumbled downstairs to the kitchen in bathrobes playing childish kissy-grabby and talking idiot-baby-love-sex-gibberish right up to the moment Illiana placed plates of steaming waffles smothered in butter, blueberries, and whipped cream in front of them. They gobbled it down like death-camp survivors then scurried back upstairs to work it off. Illiana's shoulders slumped. Woman not go away. Maybe never go away. Was problem.

# Eight

It was a little after one o'clock on a languid afternoon. Billy was in the garage sitting in the Range Rover pretending to drive. Illiana was doing laundry. She'd just pushed the start button on the dryer when cowgirl Remy stepped into the room. Her hands were on her hips. She smiled a knowing smile. Cocked her head. The smile turned into a grin. "What's going on here?"

"Go on? Nothing go on." Illiana hoped her reply conveyed the requisite amount of curiosity and innocence.

"Come on, Illiana, girl to girl, who is he?"

"Is Drek Vanko, son of famous mobster, Victor Vanko. Is good guy."

Remy gave her head a shake. "Try again."

"Is what I say," she replied firmly.

The redhead was undeterred. "Nope. One more time."

"Why you not believe?"

"His nails, honey. Have you seen his nails? Whoa! They need work."

"Not all have good nails," said Illiana. Rather unconvincingly, though, since every mobster she'd ever seen had manicured nails buffed to a high sheen. It's something she should have thought of.

"And the haircut. Yuck! Hope he got change from the dollar."

"Was emergency haircut." The phrase just slipped out before she'd had a chance to consider why a man might need an emergency haircut. Now she was stumped.

"Right," said Remy. "Well, I'll tell you what."

"What?" asked Illiana, expecting the worst.

The redhead ran her tongue around her lips. "Illiana, it's easy to see you're in control here. Let me stick around. I'll make him happy, *and* I'll make him into anything you want—hair, nails, the works! You want a mobster? I'll do a makeover that would fool Al Capone."

Illiana stared at her. "Why you want stay?"

"He's better than I have."

Although Illiana had pegged Zim at the lowest end of the evolutionary scale and treated him accordingly, from what she knew of Remy's former boyfriend, she thought perhaps the woman had a point, but just barely. And she was bright enough to know something was amiss, smart enough to know she could profit from it, and desperate enough to try. It was an encouraging combination. "What about job?"

"Got fired." Her face morphed into disgust. "Asshole boyfriend punched the salon owner in the eye. Huh! Like a gay guy is gonna be putting the moves on me. What an idiot."

"Family?"

"My daughter's twenty, married, lives in Seattle. There's no one else. Least none I care about." She spread her hands in a sign of peace and friendship. "Listen, I know something's going on here. And I know Drek likes me, at least for a while, and I have absolutely nothing going for me where I'm at. So, no matter what it is, it's a step up. Plus, I can keep my mouth shut. I'll bet that's important to you."

"Is always good to be discreet."

Remy Torriano smiled. "Tell me what you want him to look like. I'll make it happen. When I'm through, you can decide, okay?"

Illiana hesitated, but there wasn't much to consider. "Okay, job simple. Drek not mobster. Father mobster, not Drek. He nice guy. But father gone. No one but Drek. Old enemies of father will kill and take money if think Drek not tough. So, you make Drek look like tough money. Maybe save life. Maybe Drek grateful."

Remy thought for a moment and then nodded. "Tough money it is." She turned away and left the laundry room, making a lighthearted pass through the kitchen for a snack before mounting the steps on her mission. She'd sensed tension in Illiana, and it excited her. She knew the aura of wealth emanating from the castle was wholly at odds with the reality of Drek Vanko who, after stripping away the suit, car, house, and money was clearly on a cultural level with herself, if not lower. She knew it didn't work that way. Drek had money, but he wasn't money. And he wasn't the kind to attract money. That being, she thought at least some of what Illiana had told her was true—smart, tough people would take Drek's money if they knew who he really was. She also knew knowledge is power.

Not ten minutes after their discussion, Remy came back downstairs and sought out Illiana. "I gotta get my stuff, and Drek really needs new clothes. Maybe something manufactured in this century."

"Stuff?"

"Scissors, clippers, files, hair treatment, you know. Plus, I need to change."

"I understand. Is okay. For Drek clothes go Marquette. Is bigger city, more selection. Billy will drive. And get clothes for Billy too, sport coat and casual. Do one at time, understand? Not both together." She held up a finger. "And remember, what is here is private matter. Anyone find out, is bad for Drek. Bad for you too."

The last part was stated as an open threat. Remy took it in stride. "You don't have to worry about me."

"Is good," replied Illiana. "I get Billy."

It was an hour before sunset. Remy and the boys were long back from shopping. Illy and Billy were in the library having a pre-dinner cocktail, a ritual they'd fallen into. Illiana was wearing a short black dress that showed off her legs and a purple sash around her narrow waist for a splash of color. Billy was wearing one of Vanko's long blue-gray smoking jackets over a white T-shirt and jeans. He was in mid-sentence when the door opened and in strode Zim: tan leather sandals on his feet, airy off-white cotton slacks, midnight-black polo shirt. He had a gold chain around his neck and a fake diamond pinky ring. His buffed nails glistened like polished stone, and his haircut howled success. It didn't take Illiana more than an instant to know Remy Torriano was serious about staying. Zim looked fabulous! Or at least as fabulous as a Zim-creature could look.

Billy couldn't contain his mirth. Gliding his hand over his hair as if to smooth it, he said, "Fire up some Z.Z. Top for the sharp dressed man!"

Zim's expression morphed from pseudo-suave to concern. "Is it too much?"

"Is good," said Illiana with a firm nod. "Not change anything."

Remy was standing outside the doorway waiting to hear the reaction. Satisfied all was well, she stepped into the room and flowed to Zim's side. Turning her eyes to Illiana, a lightly raised eyebrow requested approval. Illiana's lips formed a thin smile and Remy relaxed. She knew she was in, but into what? She turned to Zim and asked, "Would you like a drink, Mr. Vanko?"

"Why, yes. Cognac," he replied, easing into a brown leather club chair. "And a cigar. The day's work is done. It's time to party."

Billy wondered what day's work Zim was referring to, but he didn't want to ask. A party was fine either way.

The air outside was cool but comfortable. Billy and Zim were on the back patio leaning against the stone railing, downing shots of Beam and whispering about old times, crime that is, and of days in the joint, and drawing favorable comparisons between now and then. Somehow, fate or chance or destiny had made living in a house owned by a mob couple they'd murdered become, for lack of a better phrase, the new normal. And Remy's charms had pacified Zim to a level he hadn't experienced since experimenting with heroin. That's what it felt like, the money, the house, the woman, and all the fucking risk. And he was handling it too, big time. Zim thought it was the absolute best he'd ever felt. More than thought it, he knew it.

Illiana had prepared a spaghetti and meatball dinner to rave reviews. She didn't mind cooking. Especially since the alternative of Zim or Billy fumbling around in the kitchen was too nauseating to contemplate. And they were always appreciative, a far cry from the tongue-lashings she'd received from the old bitch and the canings from Vanko. Dead was too good for them.

She and Remy were cleaning up, Remy loading the dishwasher. At least the woman has a work ethic, thought Illiana as she wiped the table.

The door to the dishwasher closed. Remy was by her side, a half-smile on her face. "It's them, isn't it?"

Illiana's hand motion slowed as her mind raced. "What mean, them?"

"You know what I mean." The smile widened.

Illiana stopped wiping.

"Their pictures were in the paper a while back, but I didn't make the connection until this afternoon."

"What picture you talk about?"

"The only thing I can't figure is what they're doing here? And, what *you're* doing here?"

"What picture?"

"Zim Crenshaw and Billy Jardean."

Illiana's lips compressed, deciding. There were knives in a butcher-block holder on the counter, sharp ones, or she could just call Billy, but she decided to talk. "Come to office. Talk private." She walked away.

Remy grinned and followed.

Once they were in the office Illiana closed the door and got right to the point. "What you want?"

"Want what every woman wants: Money."

"How much?"

Remy shrugged. "How much is there?"

"And what you think you do for money?"

"Jesus!" she said, offended. "I just spent nine hours in the sack with a guy who thinks hygiene is a greeting. If I wanted to do that for free, I'd be back with my old boyfriend."

"So?"

"Tell me what your scam is."

"Is no scam. Drek Vanko is son of mobster. You saw how was in bar. Much respect."

"Right, and I'm Mother Teresa."

"I say is so."

"Please, it's too obvious. I'm not the brightest crayon in the box, but credit me with some intelligence."

"Is just coincidence."

"Coincidence my ass. The paper said they killed a cop. Now, they're here in Loon Haven living in someone else's house, 'cause it sure ain't theirs. The clothes in the closet and the stuff that's around says old people, different people. And if that's not enough, it says Zim Crenshaw on Drek's driver's license. I took a look while he was in the shower."

Illiana tried not to show any emotion. In spite of her effort, her posture sagged. How could he be so stupid?

She stared at the woman. "I ask again, what want?"

"You're ripping this place off, aren't you? You're Billy's girl. He's been doing time but got out and was on his way to see you when he and Zim had a problem in Gaylord. Am I getting warm?"

"Yes," said Illiana, forming a plan, "warm."

"Maybe you were working for this family, these old people, but they're away on vacation or something, and Zim and Billy came here to hide out. And since you can't stay forever, the obvious move is to strip the house and disappear. The only thing I don't understand is why you'd want Zim to play mobster? What's that all about?"

"Is backup in case anyone come. Old man who live here is mobster. Bad mobster. Kill many. If friends come, must look right. Understand?'

The redhead raised a questioning finger to her lips. "Um . . . I guess."

"Must look part or we all—" Illiana pulled a finger across her throat. "Understand?"

Remy's face became serious. She understood.

"You want help? I pay."

"How much?"

Illiana sized her up. "Two thousand."

Remy coughed a laugh. "Listen honey, I should get two grand just for last night. It's gonna take a lot more than that to keep my panties off. I want a full share."

Illiana stared her in the eye. "Two is good pay for sex work."

"Is that what you think I am?"

Illiana shrugged.

"Hey, fine, think what you like, but I have Drek's

balls on a silver chain, and I can lead him anywhere I want. So put that in your pipe and smoke it."

"Maybe we go see Drek and you tell him same as me?"

"What? That he's Zim Crenshaw, ex-con, running from a murder rap? Don't get your hopes up, sweetie. He won't care if I know." Then she turned and strode out of the room, through the house, and outside onto the patio, where she snuggled up to Zim and began running her fingers up and down his crotch.

After Remy arrived, Zim's enthusiasm for conversation waned, so Billy drifted away. The sight of Illiana gazing through a kitchen window drew him inside. "Hey, babe, great meal!"

"Glad you like."

Illiana remained at the window.

"Everything okay?"

She turned to him. "Not okay, but must pretend." She smiled. "You trust me, Billy?"

"Of course," he answered, now curious.

"Here is plan. We go on porch and make sexy kissing and touching. Then we leave. Make think go bounce bed. Then I tell all. Is good with you, lover boy?"

Billy smiled. He hadn't quite picked up on what she was saying, but if it involved sexy touching, it was bound to be good. "Let's do it."

Later, upstairs, Illiana told him what had transpired between her and Remy. She said there was only one way to handle it.

# Nine

"**Z**im . . . **Zim** . . . **Zim!** . . . wake up, Illiana has breakfast ready. Bacon and eggs, don't wanna miss it."

Groggy from too much booze and an indecent amount of gymnastic sex, Zim blinked his eyes into slits.

"You too, Remy," said Billy, giving her a shake. Her body was limp. "Whoa! What's the matter here?" She was on her side. He rolled her on her back and a squit of stomach gas escaped through her mouth, a wheezing, unnatural sound.

"Zim, I think there's something wrong with Remy." Billy gave her a light slap on the cheek. "Remy! Remy! Wake up!" He grabbed her wrist, raised her arm, let it drop. It fell to the mattress and didn't move. "Zim, man, I think Remy's dead. I think you fucked her to death. Jesus, dude, you oughta put a leash on that thing."

"Wha?" Zim pushed himself up on a bony elbow and stared at the face of the dead woman next to him. "Remy? . . . Remy?" He gave her a tentative shake, quickly pulling his hand away and wiping it on the sheet. "Dead? Geez, that don't seem right."

"You have rough sex play?" asked Illiana, entering the room.

"Huh! Ah . . . no, ah, well, you know, fun rough not hurt rough."

"You do choking?"

Zim glanced at Remy's neck to validate his shaky memory. "Hell no. I'm not into that kinda kinky shit."

"Use ropes?"

"No! No ropes," he insisted.

"Cuffs?"

Frustrated. "Now where would I get a pair of cuffs?"

"Maybe choke her with mouth sex."

"I did not choke her to death with mouth sex!" replied Zim emphatically, eyes darting back and forth, searching the room for his underwear. Illiana picked his boxers off the floor and tossed them to him. This pair had honey-colored beehives circled by swarms of yellow and black bees. Considering the circumstances and all, Zim pulled them on under the covers and scuttled out of bed as if Remy Torriano's corpse were infected with the Plague. Then he stood at the bedside staring at her.

"You diddled her to death," said Billy, grinning. "You dog." He walked over to Zim and popped a congratulatory fist into his shoulder. "Bet you're hungry. C'mon, let's eat."

Illiana smiled at Zim. "Billy is right. Is time to put worries behind, food is ready. But first maybe put on clothes. His eyes went down to his naked chest, thin black hair over snowy-white skin, below it a small pot rather than a six-pack. He straightened, sucking in his gut. Illiana may be Billy's girl—as well as a skinny murderous control-freak—but she was, after all, still a woman. Collecting his shirt and pants from the floor, he followed them out of the bedroom and down the stairs to the kitchen. It was filled with the mouthwatering aroma of fried bacon.

Zim pulled on his clothes and parked his butt at the table. "Why?" he moaned, plumbing the depths of self-pity. "Why me? Geez, everything was going so well. Why'd she have to go and die?"

"Sometimes bad things happen to good people," offered Billy, stretching the limits of his knowledge of philosophy. Then he sprang back with, "Shit happens." That got a nod from Zim, as well as an "Is true," from Illiana. As she dished scrambled eggs onto their plates, Billy asked, "What do you think we oughta do with her?" Then he dug into his breakfast.

"Is good question," said Illiana, placing the pan on the counter and taking a seat at the table. "Cannot keep here. But no matter where put, have problem."

Zim swallowed a mouthful of eggs, washing it down with black coffee. "What problem?"

"Friends not hear from Remy, they start look. Last time seen, she with you. People at bar think you Vanko. Friends find name in phonebook, find address, they come, maybe bring cops. Cops not stupid, they sense problem, they watch, then we in trap with no escape."

Zim tensed.

"Won't happen today," Billy added, "but tomorrow or the next, who knows?"

A groan came out of Zim. He squeezed his eyes shut,

rubbing them with a thumb and finger to force away the nightmare of extended incarceration. "We gotta get outta here."

"Yes," said Illiana. "But first—" She was cut off by a rapping at the door.

Zim went electric. "Jesus, not already! Billy, where's the Glock?"

Billy sat there calmly. "Zimmy, it's just the door. I heard a mower earlier. It's probably the gardener."

"Billy, you and I handle," said Illiana, pushing her chair out and standing up. "Zim, go in pantry so no one see. Not worry, Billy and I make up story."

Once they were at the door, Illiana gazed through the peephole. "Is Kettleman. I will get rid." She unlocked the bolt and opened the door. "Good morning, Mr. Kettleman."

"I'm here to see Vanko, is he in?"

"Not here now but back later. What about you want see?"

"I'd better wait and talk to him directly."

"I am personal secretary. No secrets. If problem, you can tell."

"No, no, nothing like that. More of an opportunity, something we can both profit from."

Illiana smiled and nodded. "Four o'clock is good for Mr. Vanko. He be here. You come see."

"Four is fine," replied Kettleman.

As they reentered the kitchen, Billy called out, "You can come out now."

Zim appeared in the pantry doorway, a butter knife

clutched in his hand. "Cops?" he asked nervously.

"Was Kettleman," replied Illiana. "He want see about business."

"Wonder who he wants offed this time?" said Billy, gazing upward as though the answer might appear on the crown molding.

"We can do," said Illiana, "but must be on way out of town. Take care of dead woman today." Zim flinched. "Tomorrow, do banking." He tensed. "Next day must do hard work, load truck." He sagged in agony. "And one more," said Illiana.

"One more what?"

"Hit."

Already on edge, Zim's body grew rigid, thinking she might mean him.

"Cannot leave, what you call dangling string."

"Loose end?" he tentatively offered.

"Yes. Not leave end loose. Must do Kettleman, too, before leave. He is only one tie us to victims."

Billy nodded at the wisdom. Damn, he loved that girl.

"Jesus H. Christ! We're gonna need a second U-Haul just for the bodies!" whined Zim. "It's too damn much! Don't you understand? Too many dead people. Too much risk. You said it yourself, Illiana, people saw us at the nightclub with Remy. We're tied to her, and she's never going to be seen again. Eventually people will put two and two together, and they'll sure as hell be knocking on our door. Listen, we gotta load up and go. I mean today, not tomorrow or next week. If we take Vanko's credit cards and I.D. we can get his money later in Montana or Mexico or Japan, at least some of it. It's not like he's gonna be makin' any withdrawals."

Illiana shook her head. "Not smart use cards on trip. Cops and mob check card spending. Find us fast, then go jail or worse."

Zim didn't want to think about what that worse might be, but he knew there'd be less chance of it happening if they were on the goddamned road instead of lazing around the house of the mob couple they murdered after they murdered the sheriff's deputy but before they murdered the cookie lady, after which they murdered Kettleman's wife and brother and all before Remy Torriano breathed her last hot breath right next to him and her corpse is still up there getting colder by the minute. Sweet Jesus in heaven! Every cop in the Northern Hemisphere is going to be after them. "Yeah, okay, can't use the cards on the trip, but that doesn't mean we shouldn't go."

"Zim, man, you gotta relax. There's no hurry. How about last night? Wasn't that sweet? When's this ever gonna happen again?"

Zim's jaw went slack thinking of the risk. A grizzly death at the hands of the outfit or life without parole, all for a few more hours of playing make-believe? "No way, Billy. We gotta go. We gotta go now. It's too risky to stay."

"Not smart leave redhead upstairs," said Illiana.

"What does it matter?"

"You put love juice in her?"

"Love juice?"

Billy sniggered.

"You not watch CSI?" she asked reproachfully.

Zim's face fell.

"When cops find, they check. They think killed by

lover . . . same lover who pick up at bar. DNA will say ZIM. That what you want?"

"Jesus, no!" He rubbed his face with his hands. "Okay, you're right, we gotta get rid of the body."

"Not in day. Night better."

"And have her lay up there all day rotting?"

"Not rot in one day, take longer."

"How long?" asked Billy.

Illiana cocked her head, thinking. "Um, probably smell bad after day. Two weeks start get gooey."

Zim was startled. "Gooey?"

To Billy's delight, Illiana went on. "Soon, bugs find. Flies, worms, other things start eat. Couple months, most of body gone, leave teeth and bones, hair, some skin."

Zim felt his breakfast churn. "Let's put her in the trunk and go for a ride. Find a side road and drag her in the woods."

Illiana was firm. "Is good plan, but must be night so no one see. Less risk. Plus, Kettleman coming at four to meet."

"Hope it's another job," said Billy.

Zim sagged.

"More money for South America."

He was speechless.

"Only eleven now," said Illiana. "Hmm . . . is plenty of time." She turned to Billy. "Maybe Zim right, best take body to woods now. Take shovels and lye. Bury in hole so no one will find."

Whatever relief Zim felt at Illiana giving in on carcass disposal was offset by his revulsion at having to carry, drag, and dump the body of a woman who only hours before had said she adored him and wanted to spend her life pleasing him in every way possible. And she was damn well proving it too! Why? Why me? "Yeah, let's do it now and get it over with."

They trudged upstairs to the bedroom and stared at the former Remy Torriano for an unusually long time.

"She doesn't look so good anymore," said Zim.

"Let's do it," said Billy, pulling the covers off the nude woman and taking a surreptitious glance before grabbing her ankles. Zim obliged by taking hold of her wrists and they lugged the body out of the room, down the hall, down the stairs, into the foyer to the front door, laying her face up on a floral print runner. While they were doing it, Illiana went to fetch the car.

Zim and Billy had just set Remy down when they heard a knocking and thought it was Illiana. Billy unlocked the door and pulled it open, then he quickly stepped outside and pulled it shut behind him. It wasn't Illiana, it was someone else.

Late fifties, work clothes, face and hands worn by a lifetime outside, it was the gardener. "Bringing the bill for the lawn work, is Mr. Vanko around?"

"He's out. I'll give it to him." Billy stuck out his hand. The guy stepped back.

"Can't. Mr. Vanko wants me to give it to him personally. Lets me know if there's something he's unhappy with." The guy frowned. "Always seems to be something. Then he knocks it off the bill."

"Don't worry. I'll take care of it for you," replied Billy, but the guy wasn't going for it.

"You sure he isn't here? He's always here. His car's

here. I saw it in the garage." At that very moment one of the garage doors rolled up and the Caddy crept out of its stall, Illiana at the wheel. "What's she doin' driving his car?"

Billy surprised himself. "I think she's going out for groceries. Steaks an' stuff."

He stared at Billy. "Mr. Vanko don't let nobody drive his car."

Putting a little hard in it to shut the guy up. "Guess he changed his mind."

The gardener slipped past Billy and opened the door a foot. "Mr. Vanko, it's me, Cully Hixon. I got your bill. You wanna talk? . . . Mr. Vanko?" He began to push it wider.

"I told you, he ain't here," said Billy, grabbing the handle and pulling it shut. "You're lettin' in flies."

"Oh, sorry," said the gardener, still staring at the door. As he turned to Billy, he forced his lips into a smile, but his eyes told a different story. "Yeah, here, you take the bill. Give it to the old man when you see him. I'd gotta be going. Work to do." Each sentence more nervous than the last.

Billy gave him a sad smile. "We gonna make this easy, or are we gonna make it hard?"

"Oh, Christ!" said the gardener, visibly shaking. "I didn't see nothing! I'm just a gardener. I'm outside. I never go inside. I didn't see nothing."

"Zim!" yelled Billy. "Zim, I need you here!"

Zim opened the door just wide enough to squeeze out. "What's up?"

Billy nodded at the gardener. "He saw."

Just then, Hixon turned and bounded down the steps and ran across the circle drive, over the lawn, in the direction of Chipmunk Lane, but he was not a fast runner. Zim horse-collared him three-quarters of the way across and brought him down hard on his back. Billy was on him in an instant, applying his tried and true double-thumb choke. It was all over in a minute. Hixon was dead. Zim stood up. "We better get a second U-Haul."

Illiana walked over and stared down at the gardener. "Why kill?"

Billy answered. "We brought Remy down and put her by the door. He opened it and saw. Had no choice."

Illiana paused before speaking, eyes searching the air for answers. "I understand." She shrugged. "Must do what must do." Billy and Zim both nodded. "Can throw in trunk with woman, bury together. Is better sleeping with company."

"Let's do it, Zimmy. I'll get the feet."

After ferrying Hixon's pickup west to the Marquette County Airport and depositing it in long-term parking, Billy and Zim sped back to the castle, picked up Illiana, and the trio motored eastbound on burial detail. Thirty minutes later they found a dirt road branching off a little used north-south thoroughfare called Forest Highway 13 that connects M-28 on the top of the peninsula to US-2 on the bottom. The side road appeared not to have been used in years. Billy turned onto it and bumped along for a hundred yards until it became impassible with brush and saplings. Illiana made them drag the bodies deep into the forest because, unlike the Vankos, these people would be missed. Remy Torriano not so soon, but the gardener by suppertime. Illiana knew he was married because he once told her his wife packed his lunch. She knew a woman who packs a man's lunch is a woman who makes him supper, and by eight or nine she'd be calling the police. They would ask who her husband's customers were, and she would know, most likely having a list with dates and times. Zim and Billy were nearly finished filling in the hole when Illiana said, "Cops will come tonight, tomorrow morning latest. Difficult to fool. Not smart to try. Must take what can and go now. Okay?"

"Damn right it's okay!" said Zim, jubilant.

Billy wasn't so happy. "How about if we just stay the night?"

Zim gasped. Illiana shook her head sadly, "Is not safe, lover boy. Do not worry, we find other place that is nice."

"Yeah, I guess that's it," he said. "I ain't never been in a place as nice as the castle, and I'm afraid if I leave, I won't never be in another."

"Not true, Billy," she said, consoling him. "You and me and Zim are going to live good, not grovel like dogs. But sometimes must give up good thing to get better. Hard to let go, but must."

"Yeah, I guess." But his heart wasn't in it.

# Ten

The burial trip took longer than planned, and they arrived back at the castle at 3:45 with only minutes to spare before the appointment with Kettleman. Climbing the steps, Zim pleaded, "Do I have to? Can't I just wear what I'm wearing?"

"Must keep image," said Illiana. "Tough mobster not wear dirty clothes to murder meeting. Is not done."

He turned to her. "So how'd you become such an expert on all this?"

Illiana placed her hands on her hips and cocked her head. "Tough-guy cousin in business. I learn is not enough to be dangerous, must look dangerous. Otherwise, no respect. If no respect, then get trouble, not money."

It made too much sense to ignore, so he gave in. "All right, gimme a couple minutes." Billy had the door open. Zim slogged past him in the direction of the staircase.

Kettleman was there at 4:00 sharp. Cheap checked sport coat over synthetic shirt and pants. Discount shoes. When Illiana opened the door, he looked her up and down. He was losing fear, showing no respect. Wife probably better off dead, she thought. "Come in. Mr. Vanko be down soon."

"That's fine," said Kettleman, entering the house. She led him into the office, lit as before, very serious. "Sit. He will be here in minute." She turned to leave.

"Why don't you stay?"

By the way he said it and the look in his eye, she knew what he meant. "What you want, Kettleman? You think I give sex while wait?"

A smile creased his face. His eyes drifted south. "I just want to be friends."

"When I want be fuck friend with farm animal, I let you know." She turned on her heel and walked out, pulling the door closed behind her.

Killing will be good, thought Illiana. Billy and Zim can hold while I do.

Zim strode into the office in his gangster garb, complete with ascot and spats, casually sliding into the leather chair behind the desk. "I understand you want to see me?"

Kettleman smiled. "Yes."

"What about?"

His smile widened. "You know that twenty-five thousand I gave you?"

"Yes?" Zim sensed problems.

"Well . . . I want it back."

It was Zim's turn to smile. "You can't be serious?"

"One hundred percent serious."

Zim smirked. "Well, that sure as hell ain't gonna happen."

"I think it will."

"Are you on drugs, Kettleman? I oughta charge you an extra five for being a nuisance."

"Sure."

"Damn right," said Zim. "So fork over what you owe or get ready for a visit from the Squid."

"No," said Kettleman, correcting him. "You give me back the twenty-five I gave you plus an additional five for being rude."

"Are you fucking crazy? I'm a killer. Other killers work for me. We kill people like you. We do it for money, and we do it for fun, and I haven't killed anyone in, oh, gosh, going on sixteen hours now, so I'm gettin' kinda restless."

"Right," responded Kettleman dismissively. "You've probably never killed anyone in your entire life. Always had other people do your dirty work for you."

"I have so," said Zim, defensively. "I've killed lots of people. I do it all the time to stay in shape. Helps keep the weight down."

"I'm sorry, Mr. Vanko," said Kettleman. "I haven't been completely forthright."

"That's better," said Zim.

"The truth is, I want a hundred thousand dollars, and I want it by tonight, and if I don't get it or if something happens to me, there are recordings and video tapes that will be automatically mailed to various state and federal prosecuting attorneys who will, I imagine, soon be in touch with you regarding three unsolved murders. *Comprende?* You see, Vanko, what we have here is a game of chicken. Who'll blink first? Me or you? And the difference is this: You have a great life and I have a crappy one. That means you have more to lose than I do. That means I win."

"Recordings? Video? Of what? You got squat, Kettleman."

He grinned. "You should have done your homework, Vanko. What do I do for a living?"

Zim shrugged. "Who the fuck cares?"

"I sell security systems to businesses. Some are large and obvious. Others are very small."

"You recorded our conversations?"

"Of course."

"And you had a camera on you?"

"Yup, filmed it. High resolution. And if you're guessing that I had audio and video recording devices all over my house, you'd be right. I didn't get Mrs. Zumwalt's murder, of course, since I can't have a camera in every damned house in town, but I did get every single second of what they did to my wife . . . *and* to my brother." His jaw tightened. "I loved my brother, Vanko. That was a big mistake. A very big mistake."

Zim was calming down, thinking. At first he'd wanted to keep up the act, push Kettleman, scare him with threats. Then he'd wanted to jump out of his chair and add a new stain to the blade of the tomahawk. But Kettleman was right about one thing, Zim really didn't have a taste for murder. Fortunately, he knew two people who did. "Hmm, well, yeah, I guess you do have me over a barrel. All right, a hundred thou', I'll get it for you."

Kettleman was flushed with power. "One more thing, Vanko."

"What's that?"

"Send in the skinny Russian bitch. And take your time coming back."

"She's Ukrainian, not Russian. She spits on Russians."

"I don't give a damn if she's from Uranus, I'm going to teach her some respect."

Zim nodded. "Good idea."

"Get your thumbs in there," said Billy. He had Kettleman's arms pinned to the hallway floor, Zim had his legs, Illiana was sitting on his chest with her hands wrapped tightly around his throat. She'd already forced him to divulge that the recordings were in his mailbox with the flag up and the originals were in his house, so there was no virtue in delay. Kettleman's eyeballs were bulging, mouth wide, tongue flicking like a serpent, spittle running down the side of his cheek. She was pulling and pushing, pounding his balding head against the floor. "More thumbs," urged Billy. "Cut off his air." He was a professional and knew what he was talking about. A brief minute later Kettleman's eyes rolled back. He was dead.

"Oh Christ, not another body," complained Zim, dragging himself to his feet. "I'm tired and I don't feel like digging."

"What do you think, hon? What should we do?" asked Billy.

Illiana let out a breath. "Throw in big lake. Leave car nearby." The men nodded. "Afterward, go Kettleman house. Get evidence." A sly smile appeared on her face.

"And maybe leave cookie recipe for cops."

It took them a moment to recognize the brilliance of her plan, then Billy smiled. Zim smiled too.

An hour later they were back in the kitchen fixing a snack when Illiana said, "Is 5:30. I am thinking gardener's wife waiting for him come home. Soon getting worried. Must get ready to leave. Must be smart, wipe fingerprints so no one know we here."

The men agreed, and when they were through eating they pulled on rubber gloves and set to work wiping down every surface they might have touched. That took the better part of an hour. They then loaded up as much loot as they could fit in the Caddy's trunk.

By 7:00 P.M. they were ready to roll. Illiana and Zim were in the kitchen packing food for the road. They were hoping to drive straight to Bemidji in one shot. Billy drifted out to the back patio. He was leaning against the stone railing staring at the garden when Illiana opened the door and poked her head out, cheerfully calling, "Is time to go, lover boy!" But Billy was anything but cheerful. Even Kettleman's murder hadn't cheered him. He didn't want to leave and had been feeling down ever since Illy and Zim decided they should.

"What wrong?" asked Illiana, strolling up to his side. A slender hand began rubbing his back. "Not want go?"

Billy shook his head.

"Is nice here."

Billy nodded, bit his lip.

"You not before have nice." She said it with compassion.

"No."

"You think if go then not have again?"

He nodded.

She wrapped her thin arms around him and hugged him. "Not worry. You and I, Billy, we will live good. Get Vanko's money. Have nice place soon. I make sure. Is more money too. I tell about it in car, okay?"

He sighed. "You really think we can have a place this nice?"

"Is not problem. You and I, Billy, we can have good life together, if you want?"

"Oh yeah, babe, of course."

"You are good man. You deserve best."

He smiled. "I already have the best." He gazed one last time at the lush garden and then took Illiana's hand and walked to the house.


"Who want drive?" asked Illiana. They were in the garage, car packed, garage door open.

"Billy's the best," said Zim truthfully.

Billy nodded.

"Shotgun," said Zim, as if he had to since the smallest always ends up in the middle. After Billy pulled out of the garage, Illiana pushed the button on the remote and the door slid shut. Then she ran through a mental checklist: All personal items packed and in the car, bedding washed clean of DNA, every surface wiped of prints, small high-value items taken with them, no bodies lying around. She guessed that was it. Ready to roll. "Let's go."

Billy turned right at the end of the driveway onto Chipmunk Lane. He cruised at a safe speed to the junction with M-28 and stopped at the sign, waiting for a line of westbound cars to pass before entering the highway. The last one slowed. It was a cop. He was turning onto Chipmunk Lane. "Fuck a duck," said Billy under his breath.

"Stay cool," said Zim, as nervous as a porcupine in mating season.

"Not worry," said Illiana. "They not look for us . . . yet." The yet part caused Zim's blood pressure to spike.

Billy stayed put. The cop made the turn. Stared at them as he did. Zim and Billy stiff as boards, Illiana pretending to chatter as though it were a normal drive. The cop passed. Billy kept his head straight, but his eyes were glued to the mirror. "He's slowing down. He's stopping."

"Turn on road and drive away," urged Illiana.

"Too late. He's backing up."

The cruiser pulled back next to the Caddy. The officer rolled down his window. Billy just sat there, head turned, staring at him, didn't move. Frustrated, the cop made a rolling motion with his hand. "Must put down window," said Illiana prompting. Billy did it. Stared at the cop. Zim had the Glock. Billy hoped if push came to shove he wouldn't get shot in the exchange.

"Do you know which house belongs to the Vankos?" asked the cop.

Billy took a deep breath, didn't respond.

"Is third on left," said Illiana. "Look like big castle."

"Thanks," said the cop. Billy was still staring at him. The cop stared back, nodded. "Have a nice evening." Then his car began moving up Chipmunk Lane toward the castle.

Billy made the turn onto M-28 and brought the Caddy up to the exact speed limit, 55.

Illiana said, "Cop not find anything at house. Lights off, door locked, no one home. Him not break in for no reason. And if do, so what? We clean up good, no trace."

"But he saw us," said Zim. "They probably got pictures circulating everywhere."

"What? Bad jail picture? You not look in mirror? Look sharp, dress sharp, ride in sharp car, no one suspect unless you show nervous, then wonder, otherwise no." Illiana turned on the radio and punched buttons until a country song with a solid beat pulsed through the speakers. Billy was getting in the mood. "Road trip!" he howled, then he barked like a coyote.

"Road trip!" echoed Illiana.

Zim raised his hands in defeat, a victim of optimism. "Road trip."

# Eleven

After missing a critical turn due to Zim's inattention as navigator, three hours later and nearing ten o'clock Billy was hungry, so they stopped at an eatery called the Ambassador in the town of Houghton. Even with the extra miles from the map-reading error, in another two hours they'd be out of Michigan. And after a short stretch in Wisconsin, they'd be in Minnesota, two states away from the murders, two states safer. When the check came, Zim reached into his pocket. Then he froze, eyelids closed, mouth clamped shut, mind deep in thought. Illiana noticed.

"What is wrong?"

Zim swallowed hard. "I left something."

That got Billy's attention. "What?"

His head bent forward in agony. "My driver's license."

"Illiana's eyes doubled in size. "How could you do such?" she hissed. "Is like story of dumb criminal on news."

Zim twisted away, a dog cowering from an angry master. "I didn't mean to. I . . . I hid it to be safe . . . and then I forgot it in the rush to leave."

"Where is?" she asked. "On dresser?"

Zim got a little spine back. "*No,* it's not on the dresser. I hid it under the mattress."

"Is clever. Cops would never think to look."

"All right, I screwed up. But it doesn't matter because we gotta keep going."

She shook her head. "Must go back."

"What? That's nuts."

"Fine. You get room, stay here. Billy and I go back."

"Cool," said Billy. "Back to the castle!" He was jazzed, never wanted to leave in the first place.

With Zim comfortably ensconced in a nearby Super 8, Billy wheeled the Cadillac southeast and back toward Loon Haven. Knowing Zim was out of her life for at least a few hours, Illiana relaxed, sliding over to Billy's side and tucking her arm under his.

The radio was low and moody, and the Caddy was purring. Billy felt like king shit. They were on their way back to the castle. Shoulda never left. It was too good to leave. Well, at least they'd spend the night and he'd have Illiana again in that huge bed. It was like being in heaven. And since throughout his life people had assured him that he wasn't going to the real heaven, he thought it'd be best to grab as much as possible right here, right now, and let the memory comfort him later on, wherever he may be.

"Billy, let us think."

Her words got his attention.

"Only Kettleman know we do cookie lady, right?"

Billy thought for a moment. "Right."

"Same with Kettleman wife and brother."

Billy nodded. It was pretty easy thinking.

"And no one but us know about Kettleman and gardener."

"Right."

"So, is only two problems: gardener and redhead."

Billy nodded again. "Yup."

"If cops come ask about gardener, can say did job, gave bill, left. What happen after that, we not know. Why they suspect more?"

Billy didn't know.

"And if ask about redhead, can say she and Zimdrek run off on sex trip to island? Is something friends would believe."

Billy sniggered at the thought of Zim on an island fuck trip, his snow-white skin being seared by the blazing tropical sun while he lay on a sandy beach in sweaty exhaustion. Then the full impact of what Illiana was saying hit him. "Wow!" He smiled, totally in awe of such a brilliant plan. A feeling of pure glee coursed through him at the prospect of staying in the castle for more than one night. Oh god, Illiana was brilliant! And, she was his. "Man, this is cool." He gave the Caddy a goose and felt the acceleration push him back in his seat.

Illiana smiled. "So maybe is good idea for Zim to visit friends in Minnesota. Stay out of sight."

"Yes," replied Billy, totally convinced.

Illiana gave it some thought and then said, "Must go

back to motel, explain plan to Zim. Must give share of money, otherwise problems."

"Go back?"

"Must do, lover boy, otherwise Zim upset. Maybe think bad thoughts, make problem."

Billy's lips compressed. "Dang! I suppose." He began to slow the car.

"What?" Zim was lying on one of the beds, propped against a pile of pillows with a bottle of Johnny Walker Black in his hand, already having done some sipping in their absence.

"Is good plan," said Illiana. "Billy and I stay at castle till get Vanko's money. Better to do from there. Go bank, if must."

"Who? Him?" He waved the bottle at Billy.

Billy sensed the slight and straightened. "I can do it."

"Of course can," said Illiana, calming him. "Dress up, say right thing, easy."

"He don't look old enough," said Zim.

Illiana shrugged. "I fix."

The thought of splitting up filled Zim with dread. Naturally, the first thing he thought about was the money. "What about my share?"

Illiana said, "That why we come back." Billy pulled a roll of cash from a pocket and handed it to him. Illiana continued, "Is eight thousand."

"What about my share of the stuff in the car?"

"Not sold yet. When sold, we split."

Zim was calming down. "And what about my share of the million?"

"No problem. You give address of friends. When get money, we come. All three go Argentina, be safe, live good."

Zim looked at Billy. Billy nodded. "It's a good plan, Zim."

Billy and Illy pulled into the driveway well after midnight, the castle brooding, backlit by a full moon. They'd left one light on in the foyer. The soft glow could be seen through beveled-glass on either side of the door. Stopping in front of the house, Billy shut off the engine. With Illiana trailing, he strode to the door, unlocked it and stepped inside. He began to say something but stopped when Illiana grabbed his arm.

"What?" he whispered.

She pointed to a black leather jacket hanging on the rack by the door. Billy's brow knitted. He couldn't remember if it was there before. Probably not. The Glock was in the glove compartment of the Caddy. He held up a finger signaling 'wait' then turned and went out the door, returning moments later bearing a more confident demeanor. "What now?"

"We check house. I go in front."

Billy nodded, and he and Illiana quietly began checking all the rooms on the first floor. Not finding anyone, they crept up the staircase and began scouring the second.

They found him in a spare bedroom. They couldn't see him, but they could hear him snoring. Billy switched on the light. He was lying in the bed. Long black hair, swarthy complexion, Billy sized him up as tough but doable. The guy didn't even wake up. To Billy's astonishment, Illiana walked directly up to the sleeping man and gave him a hard whack on the head. "Wake up, Alexei Petrovich, you son of pigs, and get ready to die!"

"You know him?" asked Billy, confused.

"Yes," said Illiana. "Is one who sold me to Vanko."

It was difficult information to process. He had never really wondered how she'd gotten to the castle. What did it matter? He relaxed. The man was not a rival, not someone of any consequence, other than being at the very top of the Squid's to-do list.

Alexei Petrovich sat up in bed, brushing strands of hair from his face. Billy noticed he was muscled up, tats all over, and went jailhouse hard at the possible threat.

Petrovich said, "Is that any way to treat a cousin?"

"Don't talk of cousin," said Illiana, her words cutting like a razor. She turned to Billy. "This is man who sell me like dog."

Billy frowned. "That pisses me off. Want me to do him?"

Petrovich's eyes grew wide. "No, Illiana, my little Bukovina buttercup, you have wrong. I did not sell, I only loan as collateral for debt. Just temporary. Now I have money to pay Vanko, bring you home to Chicago. I make appointment two weeks ago. I come, door open, no one here, so I come in and wait."

"You lie. Door not open."

"Back door. Why care? Vanko not mind. I come to pay."

"You bring money?"

"Of course."

"Where is?"

He hesitated. Billy lifted the Glock, pointing it at his gut. "In pants pocket."

"How much?" asked Illiana.

"Nine hundred," he said sheepishly. "Lost in poker game."

Illiana's mouth opened in shock. "Nine hundred dollars? You sell me to Vanko, make me work here like animal for five months, you only owe nine hundred dollars and not pay till now?"

"Is lot of money, Illiana. I have business to run. Takes cash. Cannot stop business." He shrugged. "Anyway, what is problem? I am here now." He glanced at Billy. "Tell fancy boy to put down gun."

Fancy boy? thought Billy. Wouldn't that be something like a punk? Billy set the gun on the dresser nearest the door and flexed his fingers. Nobody calls Billy the Squid a fancy boy.

The guy was tough but Billy was in a zone, a human killing machine, a professional. The fight only lasted a minute, but by the time it was over they were on the floor. After choking the life out of him, Billy gave him a couple of hard shots to the face just to let him know he was pissed, and so he'd remember not to go selling people again in heaven, or wherever he was going.

After he'd rushed the bed and begun pounding on Petrovich, Illiana acted as his fight manager. "Good, Billy, good! Break nose so can't breathe! Gouge eye! Yes! Pull finger back, hard. Elbow, Billy, elbow to face! Yes, yes, yes! Thumbs, Billy, more thumbs!" When it was over Billy stood up, rolled his neck, and brushed himself off. He felt on top of the world.

Illiana said, "Good work, lover boy. Ride make me hungry. You want eat?"

Billy nodded. "What about the body?"

"Wrap in blanket and push under bed. We deal with tomorrow. But must eat quick."

"Why quick?"

She displayed a coquettish smile. "Afterward, I give hot sex present to Billy the Squid."

"Yum," he said and followed her down the stairs.

After eating, they had wild sex in the big four-poster bed. Later, they were lying together in an easy perfection, moments from sleep, when Illiana tensed. "Billy!" she whispered. "I hear noise!"

# Twelve

Silvery moonlight cascaded through the windows. Shadows moved on the walls. The Glock was on the nightstand. Billy picked it up, slid out of bed, padded to the door, Illiana behind him. He put his ear to it and listened. Then he stepped back. "Why don't you stay here, babe. Don't want you to get hurt."

She shook her head. "Where you go, I go."

"All right, but stay behind me." He reached for the knob, turned it, slowly opened the door and then stopped. "Someone's singing . . . I think it's 'House of the Rising Sun.' "

"Him not good singer," whispered Illiana.

"It's the high notes. They don't sound right."

"Maybe can help."

They stepped into the dimly lit hallway. The voice was coming from one of the other bedrooms. Billy hoped it wasn't the room Petrovich was in. That would be creepy.

They quietly tread their way down the hall. All the

way to the end. The last bedroom. That's where the sound was coming from. There was someone inside singing "House of the Rising Sun." Loudly, badly, as if he were drunk. "Let's do it," said Billy as he grabbed the doorknob, flung open the door, and stepped inside, gun high. The singing continued, louder now that he was in the room. It was coming from the bathroom. Billy could hear water running. The guy was taking a shower. This was going to be easy.

He tiptoed across the room, Illiana close behind. The bathroom door was ajar, shower running hot, steam escaping from the opening.

*"And it's been the ruin of many a poor boy."*

Billy pushed the door open and they stepped into a white-tiled room, double sinks with gold fixtures, porcelain clawfoot tub with a shower curtain hanging from a ring, room thick with steam.

*"And God, I know I'm—"* The singing stopped abruptly when Billy ripped down the shower curtain.

Blond hair, medium build, rugged but friendly face. "Jesus!" said the man, squeezing the bar of soap in his hand so tightly that it shot out and hit Illiana in the pubic region.

Billy straightened. "Fuck you think you're doin', butthead, throwin' your soap at my girl?"

"Yo, man, be cool, it slipped. You caught me by surprise. Hey, dude," he said, with a boozy drawl. "Why not lay down the tool an' come on in?" His smile stretched ear to ear. He cocked his head. "You know, you two don't have any clothes on." He stared at Billy, longer at Illy.

"Hey, fuckwad! Keep your eyes to yourself."

"Yo, man," he whined, "she don't have no clothes on. Ain't that many women comfortable enough with their bodies to walk up on a stranger in a bathroom without any clothes on." Glancing back at Illiana, he nodded. "You're okay." He smiled again, and then his eyes went from one to the other. "You guys wanna come in?" The invitation hung in the air. "It's nice, you know. Rub-a-dub-dub, three friends in a tub?"

Billy glared at him. "What is wrong with you?"

"Wrong? Nothing. You guys wanna get high?"

"What you do here?" asked Illiana, hands on hips.

"I'm here with Petrovich."

"Shoot him."

Billy raised the Glock.

The man leaned back defensively. "Jesus, no! What are you gonna do that for?"

Illiana said, "Your boss is scum. That mean you scum."

"Whoa! Wait a minute. Petrovich ain't my boss. I hardly know him. His car broke down and I gave him a ride. Said he'd pay me a hundred bucks to drive him here. Said I could spend the night. Part of the deal. But I don't work for him. No, no, no. Never saw him before in my life till tonight, so there ain't no call to shoot me. I'm a lover, not a fighter." He could see Billy hesitating. "Man, wouldn't you rather party? I got some good weed . . . and some 'shrooms . . . even a little coke. C'mon, guys, whatever you got going here ain't none of my business. I'm just passing through. Can't we be friends?"

Billy said, "Don't look at my girl."

The man's eyes went to the ceiling, the wall, the

ceiling. "It's kinda hard when she's standing right in front of me with no clothes on."

"Well, pretend she has clothes on," said Billy.

Illiana glanced at him and her brow furrowed.

"Sure," said the dude. "No problem." He lowered his eyes and stared straight at her hoo-ha. "That's a nice dress you have on."

"I'm gonna kick your ass," said Billy, handing the Glock to Illiana.

"Whoa, man!" hands up in a gesture of peace, "I was just doin' what you told me."

Billy backed off.

"What is name?" asked Illiana.

"Oz, hon. Everyone calls me Oz. And, you know, if you guys ain't gonna get in the shower, maybe we'd better get some clothes on. I don't want Mister Potato Head to have a misunderstanding about what's going on here." He pointed to his dick.

"Give me the gun," said Billy.

Oz's eyebrows went up. "Wait, wait! You guys wanna stay naked, that's your business. I'm not trying to stop you. Hell, go downtown and dance on a car if you like, it's nothing to me."

"You not know Petrovich?" questioned Illiana.

He shook his head vigorously. "Told you. Never met him before tonight."

"Did he pay?"

"Said he'd do it tomorrow before I left."

"Alexei Petrovich is scum. Would not have paid."

Oz's face fell. "Really? Oh, man, now I'm screwed." His shoulders slumped.

"Why screwed?" asked Illiana.

"I ain't got enough gas to get home."

"Where's home?"

"Marinette."

"Where is Marinette?"

"'Bout halfway to Green Bay on the Wisconsin side of the border."

Illiana gazed into his eyes. "If we give money, you can drive home?"

Oz's face registered surprise. "Ah . . . well . . . I ain't got no clothes on . . . and I just smoked some bitchin' bud . . . and I put a pretty good dent in a six-pack since I got here, but . . . ah . . . (he glanced at the Glock back in Billy's hand) . . . yeah, I think I can drive."

"Where is car?"

"Petrovich had me put it in the garage."

"He's fucked up," said Billy. "He's gonna get in an accident."

"I don't wanna get in an accident, man. Don't wanna hurt no one. C'mon, how 'bout we party a little, then I sleep, then I go?"

"It'd be safer," said Billy, highway safety being of concern to him.

Oz brightened, "Maybe Alexei wants to party too?"

"Is sleeping. Must not wake," replied Illiana.

"Well then, just the three of us. I got some good bud. It's sativa, man. Blue Dream."

Billy shrugged. "Wouldn't mind a taste of good bud."

So it was settled.

Oz asked, "You guys wanna shower first? It's okay, you can come in."

"Don't push it," said Billy. "Get some clothes on and meet us downstairs in the library. It's the room with the books."

"Cool," said Oz, leaning over and grabbing a towel from a rack. He wrapped it around himself then carefully stepped out of the tub and half walked, half staggered into the bedroom toward his clothes scattered on the bed.

Illy and Billy followed him into the bedroom and began to leave, but Illiana stopped. Oz noticed. "You gonna watch?"

"Already seen naked. Not hurt watch put on clothes."

Oz gave a strained smile, did a quick dry-off, then dropped the towel to the floor and began dressing. Briefs, pants, shirt, socks, and shoes went on quickly. He glanced at his jacket lying on the dresser but didn't reach for it. "I'm ready."

Illiana stared at him. "Pick up jacket. Do slow."

Billy was alert, the palm of his hand sensing the knurled handle on the Glock.

"My jacket? What do I need that for?"

"Can get cold in library."

Fucker's got a gun in his jacket, thought Billy, upset with himself for not checking but ready for whatever came.

Oz hesitated, then reached for it. As he pulled it off the dresser, Illy and Billy could see it had weight in a pocket. Billy's gun hand came up. "Toss it over."

"Oh man, ain't nothin'. Up here lots of people have guns. Everyone really." He tossed the jacket toward Billy. It fell to the floor with a slapping thud. Illiana picked it up and went through the pockets, pulling out a small black .22.

"Is hitter's gun."

Oz's mouth opened. "Hitter? No, no, you got me wrong. I'm a lover, not a fighter."

Billy said, "Then what you doin' with a hitter's gun?"

"It's not!" he pleaded.

Illiana said, "You think maybe we stupid? Gun have tape on handle and trigger so no prints. Shoot .22 to back of head, not loud, small hole, not much blood, bullet bounce in skull, make mush, dead before hit ground. So, I ask again, why you have hitter's gun? Billy will shoot in leg if not answer."

Billy smiled and nodded.

"Alexei gave it to me. I swear. He gave it to me as a gift, you know, because of the ride."

"Shoot him," said Illiana.

Billy pulled the trigger. It was followed by a loud bang and a yowl of pain from Oz as he crumpled to the floor.

"Jesus Christ! That was unnecessary," he said, compressing the bloody hole in his left thigh. "It's just a job, okay? Yes, I work for Petrovich, but I'm not a hitter, I'm a bodyguard. Okay? So be cool, all right? It's just a job, it ain't nothing to be killing a guy over."

Illiana said, "You not much good at bodyguard work."

Oz looked puzzled. Then realization dawned. "Petrovich is dead? Oh, shit!"

Illiana handed the .22 to Billy and asked for the Glock. He gave it to her.

Afterward, they rolled the body into a blanket to soak up the blood then slid the bundle under the bed. Lots of work for tomorrow, thought Billy. "I'm kind of awake now. Wanna make some popcorn and see if there's a movie on?"

Illiana nodded. Still naked as jays, they padded out of the room in the direction of the kitchen.

# Thirteen

**Z**im lay semi-reclined on the bed in the Super 8, sipping Johnny Walker and clicking through channels until he became bored. Ignoring an admonition from Illiana about going out, he slipped on his loafers, grabbed his jacket and made for the door. Driving to the motel, he'd noticed a nightclub nearby. He was lookin' sharp. He had a fat roll. He was the Zimdrek. He already had a room, all he needed was the lady.

She worked him over good. Boozed him up at the bar with hints of something special after they'd had a few, and then waltzed him to his room and put him to sleep with a back rub.

The next morning Zim awoke with a nasty hangover and no female companionship. Though he could barely think for the throbbing in his head, it didn't take long for his spirits to sag even lower. His pants were on the floor. He checked the pockets. They were empty.

He was in a strange town, no money, no friends, and wanted by every law enforcement agency in the Midwest. The Zimdrek had arrived, but the destination was all fucked up. He pulled on his clothes and shuffled into the bathroom. He gazed at himself in the mirror, grimaced, splashed water on his face, toweled it off, poked at a possible zit. Thoroughly disgusted, he went back and sat on the edge of the bed trying to sort it out. What the hell am I gonna do? I can't go to Minnesota like this. No money and nothing to offer in exchange for being put up. Pruno and Shank are friendly, but they ain't that friendly. Shank in particular. They'd be pissed if I showed up busted and on the lamb with nothing to give 'em for takin' the risk of having me there. Heck, them boys might start thinkin' there's reward money to be had in exchange for my hide. That shit damn well ain't gonna work. I got no choice. I gotta go back to the castle. Just then, there was a knock on the door. Zim panicked. Glancing around, he realized the lone window didn't open wide enough for him to crawl out. Anyway, he was on the second floor and wasn't keen on a fifteen-foot drop onto concrete or prickly bushes or whatever. Maybe if he kept quiet they'd go away.

Tap, tap, tap. "Zim?"

It wasn't the cops, it was his hot money-thieving honey from the previous night. His brow furrowed. That can't be right?

"Zim, baby, open up. It's me, Lolly."

Lolly, right. She'd said it was short for lollypop. "Lolly, yeah sure. Hang on a second. He stepped back into the bathroom, used water on fingers to slick back his hair, rinsed out his mouth, toweled off the excess, tucked in his shirt, and went to the door.

"Good to see you're up and taking nourishment, sweetie," said Lolly in a singsong voice. She was a chesty woman in her fifties with big hair, a tiny waist, and thunder thighs. Her fire engine nails and midnight makeup bluntly proclaimed 'I have no taste.' She gave him a peck on the cheek that left crimson marks. Zim was stunned, deeply questioning his lack of standards. "Lolly, hey, good to see you."

"I brought doughnuts," she said, gleefully pulling a box out of a shopping bag. "And coffee too."

"Doughnuts? Yum!" Brushing aside reservations, "Got any crullers? They're my favorite."

"Yeah, there's two." Smiling, "Just for you, baby."

"Aw, that's sweet." He tucked a cruller in his mouth. "But hey, what about the eight g's I had in my wallet?"

Reaching for her purse, "Got it right here for you. What's left. You were throwing it around pretty loose last night. You gave the rest to me to hold so you wouldn't spend it. Remember?"

He didn't. Nor did it seem like something he'd ever do. "How much is left?"

"Don't know, didn't count it. Here you go." She handed him a stack of bills held together by a rubber band.

Fanning the edge, he figured there was a little over seven grand left. He scowled.

"Don't be mad at me, Zimmy. I got a client for you."

"What?" A client? What the hell did I tell her?

"Wants her boyfriend whacked. Last night you said that's what you do. Ten grand, you said. You got a guy named Squid who'll do it for ten. You weren't shining me, were you? I stuck my neck out."

"No," said Zim, casually tucking the money in his pocket. "If there's a job to be done, my man can do it. But I gotta see cash up front."

"She's outside."

"What?"

"Outside the door. Her name's Gloria, but everyone calls her Rail. Okay if I bring her in?"

Zim's mind jammed, then he said, "Guess it's better than having her stand out in the hall." Yearning to add: And draw attention to my room so I'll get arrested and spend the rest of my short life in prison before being brutally murdered.

Rail fit her nickname. Tall, thin, long stringy hair of an indeterminate color, marginally attractive, but she'd been beaten lately so that made it not as good, and long sleeves on a warm day covering up god knows what. She sat on one of the two beds, Zim across from her on the other. There was no discernible expression on her face.

"So, you want him whacked. Can't blame you."

"Yeah." Dull beat-up woman voice. "Kill the fucker."

"You got the money?"

A small faux-leather purse hung by a frayed strap from her shoulder. She opened it and pulled out a wad of cash. "It's ten grand. I counted it." She held it out.

Feeling as though he'd entered an altered state, one that did not seem anywhere near healthy, Zim took it.

"The ten's from sellin' his truck, so it's gotta be done tonight else I'll be the one gets killed."

"Gotta make a call to check on availability," he said. "Booking issues."

He sidled over to the phone and pulled a piece of paper out of his pocket that had the number for the castle written on it. Since Vanko was a known mobster and wire-taps on known mobsters are common practice, Illiana had expressly warned against calling. Nevertheless, pride and money were at stake. He dialed the number. The phone rang. To his deep disappointment, Illiana answered.

"Vanko residence."

"Illiana, it's me. Billy around?"

"What you want him for?"

"It's a job."

"Not say more. You at same place?"

"Yes."

"I call back."

"When?"

"Soon." She hung up.

Zim produced a salesman's smile. "Looks like there might be an opening."

In her dead voice, Rail said, "He's a choker, right?"

Zim was thrown. "Yeah, sure, a choker."

"'Cause that's what I want. Choke the prick to death, just like he tried to do me."

"No problem," said Zim, reeling from the hate. "My guy's a choker. That's what he does. It's his specialty."

"Is he big?"

He shrugged. "Big, but not real big."

"The Crowbar's big."

"How big?"

"'Bout two-ninety. And he's mean. So your choker better be prepared. Just sayin'."

He rubbed his chin. "The Squid's tough, but as you can imagine, in our business we ain't lookin' for no fair fight. Would you be opposed to us shooting him once or twice to soften him up before the choking?"

"If you shoot him, the choking won't be as miserable."

"I'm not saying shoot him bad. Just once or twice in the legs to get him down, that's all. Then the choking starts. And remember, that's the good part. Leg pain won't even register once the Squid wraps his tentacles around the Crowbar's throat."

"What's a tentacle?"

Marine science is woefully under-appreciated, thought Zim. "A squid has lots of arms, see?" his own arms mimicking tentacles, waving and grasping at the air.

"Fuck's that?" said Rail, recoiling.

"Hell you think it is?" replied Zim. "Tentacles. *Squid* tentacles."

"No shit? That what they're like?"

He nodded.

"Scary. If Crowbar kicks his ass, I want my money back."

"Ain't likely. The Squid's a professional. But don't worry, we guarantee our work."

"Well, hot damn," said Rail, expressionless. "He's been runnin' with his boys, but they're comin' back tonight. They'll stay at the bar till closing time, then he'll come home. Should be ridin' in 'bout two-thirty on his hog. He'll be fucked up, but don't let that fool you. He don't mind doin' some hurt."

"That where you want him killed? Right there in front of your house?"

"Don't matter to me. Ain't nobody gonna think I did it."

Zim was forced to agree. "Fine. Gimme your address. And make sure if it's north something or south something you say so."

She gave him a blank stare.

"We've had problems in the past."

Rail cocked her head. "Say, I was just thinkin'. He's got guns I could sell. How much more for dragging him through town behind a car?"

Zim realized they needed a price list. Everyone knows the real profit's in add-ons.

"Bidding custom jobs is always difficult. Hmm . . . there's extra risk in street dragging, 'cause it's not like no one's gonna notice. And it leaves a trail of blood and other stuff right to where you park. And there's the cost of the chain to think of. Add it all up, I'd probably have to charge double." He spread his hands in helplessness.

"Couldn't you use rope?"

Zim shook his head. "It's a matter of tensile strength. Can't have it breaking when he's only halfway sanded down."

Rail shrugged. "I guess I'll go for the basic choking package." Displaying her first sign of emotion, "I can't wait to watch."

Zim's eyebrows went up. "You want to watch?"

"Sure do! I want him lookin' right in my face while he's dying."

He gave a lawyerly exhale. "Rail, I can understand your zeal to be rid of the Crowbar, but you do understand that if you were to watch, the Squid would have to kill you too."

She almost smiled. "Might be worth it."

"It's not worth it. Stay in the house. Don't look outside."

"Yeah, okay. I'll leave some cookies on the porch."

Zim tensed. "Cookies? Why cookies?"

Now she did smile. Zim wished she hadn't. Meth teeth. "Everyone's heard of the Squid."

Zim shooed the women out, Lolly giving him a quick peek at one of her tits and a bloozy wink before she left. She gave her hips a grind on the way out and said she was looking forward to getting her finder's fee. Zim figured she'd gotten more than enough the previous evening, so he wasn't feeling too generous.

After they left, he waited nervously in the room for twenty minutes before the call came. Illiana started right in. "What is trouble?"

Zim's body sagged. "It's not trouble, it's a job. I got us a job here, for tonight."

"Tell about job."

"Whackin' some woman-beatin' biker."

"How you get job in motel room?"

He sighed. "Look, I got bored so I went out. I met a woman. She had a friend who needed some work done. I said we could do it, that's all. And I already got the dough."

"You got money?"

"Yes, of course. I'm the Zimdrek, remember? Money first."

"You are learning."

Zim felt a rush of pride.

"How much?"

"Ten large."

"That best can do?"

"What are you talking about? Ten's good."

"Long drive, maybe could get mileage."

"Look, I already got the cash. I can't go nickel-diming this poor woman. That's not good business. Customer satisfaction is important, you know. Referrals and all."

Illiana conceded the point. "Why tonight? What is hurry?"

"It's her old man. He's a nasty prick calls himself Crowbar. She sold his truck for the money. He's out of town, but he'll be back tonight, and if we don't whack him first, he'll do her. Then we gotta give a refund."

"No refunds," she said sternly.

"It seemed real important to her. It would have been a deal-breaker. I had to agree."

"Okay, fine. We do tonight."

Zim hesitated. "There's one more catch, well, two. The dude's big. And he's mean. So it makes sense to pump some lead into him before the *coup de grâs*."

"*Coup de grâs*? What is *coup de grâs*?"

"It's German for kick his ass."

"Is not German. Is French."

"You don't even know what it means, so how do you know it isn't German?"

Illiana emitted a low growl. "What is point of *coup de grâs* talk?"

"The point is, Miss Smarty Pants, the customer is looking for a good choking. She's all lathered up to have the Squid do his tentacle thing. That in particular. She's even leaving cookies. That's how excited she is. So, what we oughta do is have Billy shoot him a couple times to discourage him and then get on with the choking."

"Whoa! Tell why cookies?"

"Word's gotten out. Billy the Squid is a name hitter. The cookies are an offering."

"What? Like to shrine of baby Jesus?"

"No, don't be ridiculous. That'd be gross. It's more like a gift to say thanks for a job well done. That sort of thing."

"I am smelling trouble. Is not good to be famous. Maybe you should do?"

Zim would have no part of it. "She wants the Squid, so it's gotta be him. But look, I don't mind helping."

"Okay then. I do shooting, Billy and you do rest. Then you go Bemidji, right?"

"Damn straight."


The biker was much harder to kill than they had anticipated. Five slugs in him, one that severed a toe, and it still took both Zim and Illy to hold him down while Billy did his work. Zim noted how Billy flexed his fingers to relax them, and how he carefully approached the throat area like a surgeon about to perform a delicate operation. Then, *bam!* He'd latch on and drive those thumbs home, pounding up and down with his body in an almost sexual frenzy until the biker was absolutely, positively, beyond all doubt, dead.

Rail couldn't help herself. As soon as the shooting ended and the choking began, she ran out of her house to join the mêlée. Craning her face over the Crowbar's bug-eyed visage, she screamed, "How's that feel, motherfucker! How's that feel!" over and over until Illy told her to shut up.

After the business portion of the evening was over, Rail invited them in for a drink and some meth. They said it was late, so maybe next time, but they did take the cookies.

Rail's place was a few miles out of town. On the ride back to drop Zim at the Super 8, Illiana said, "Not good go back motel. Not good stay in town. Motel paid?"

"Yeah, paid through tonight."

"You leave anything?"

"My suitcase."

"Must get. I am thinking bus here not good. We should drive you Green Bay. Take bus from there."

Zim sighed. "Sure, fine, whatever you like. But I want to take a chunk of this fresh cheese along with me. I'm thinking Pruno and Shank will be a lot friendlier if I keep the party going."

"How big cheese chunk you want?"

"Just my third. Call it traveling money."

"Mister Big Spender is going to last maybe one week and then be in jail."

"Not gonna happen," argued Zim.

Billy said, "I'm a little tired. Don't know if I can make it all the way to Green Bay. It's only an hour and a half back to the castle. Why not go there and get a good night's sleep and drive to Green Bay in the morning?"

"Is fine with me," said Illiana.

"Go back?" A shiver went through Zim. "Too many bodies in Loon Haven. Something bad's gonna happen. Maybe Vanko's chums, maybe the cops, either way I don't want to be a part of it."

"How about we drop you Marquette? Catch bus Green Bay in morning?"

"Yeah, okay, sounds like a plan," he replied, relieved.

Billy chuckled. "Anyway, we got guests."

Zim gave a questioning glance. "Guests?"

"Yeah, stopped by last night. They're resting now."

"Resting?"

"We wrapped 'em up and shoved them under the beds. Slept late this morning and then you called and after thinking about it, we thought we'd better unload the Caddy rather than risk driving around with the stuff and, well, we didn't have time to clean up. Had to do 'em, Zimmy."

Zim was in a dither. "Who? Who came to the castle last night that you had to kill?"

"Someone from Chicago named Petrovich, and a hitter called himself Oz. Illiana knew Petrovich."

"You whacked someone from the Chicago mob?"

"Yup, that's what happened."

"Marquette's fine. Drop me there."

But by the time they got to Marquette, Zim was snoring, so Billy drove on through."

"Zimmy, wake up. We're home."

A groggy Zim came to life. Realizing where he was, his head drooped. The castle of doom. He couldn't get away.

"You and Illiana were sleeping, man. Just made more sense to come straight home."

"Yeah," said a dejected Zim.

They left the car in front and unlocked the heavy door. When they stepped inside, Zim's nose curled. "Something stinks."

"Bodies," said Illiana. "Should have disposed this morning."

"Bad decision. Anyone comes to the door, cops, mob, anyone, they'll know we got bodies."

"Must move now," said Illiana.

Billy said, "I know you're right, hon, but I'm tired."

"How 'bout drag downstairs, put in trunk of car, deal with in morning."

Billy and Zim agreed it was the most practical thing to do, them being tired and all but not wanting to sleep with the smell. Twenty minutes later they were done and Illiana had the place aired out.

The next morning found them sitting around a sunny breakfast table discussing what to do with the bodies.

"How about in the woods with Cully and Remy?" offered Billy. "Give 'em some company."

"Ain't smart to go back the same place," opined Zim. "Some other place in the forest, that's what I'm thinking."

"Sure. I'll go load up the shovels."

Billy walked to the front door, opened it, stepped out onto the granite porch and stopped in his tracks. "Zim!" he called. "Zim! I need you to come here. The car's gone."

# Fourteen

**B**ack in the kitchen, Zim popped open a post-breakfast beer. "Some prick stole it. Some prick stole our goddamned car from right in front of our house. Damn! You can't trust nobody." He guzzled half the brew. "Fucking surprise in store for him if he gets pulled over." He emitted a croaking laugh and chugged the rest, crushing the can with his hand to express his rage.

Illiana said, "Then cops look for owner."

"That's not good," said Billy.

Zim said, "By now those bodies must be stinking bad. Won't take much brainpower to realize the smell's coming from the trunk. Wish I could see the mook's face when he opens it." He huffed a laugh. "Can't imagine any car thief wanting a part of that. He'll abandon it. Then the cops will find it. One second later there'll be a hundred squad cars rolling our way."

"Must find," said Illiana. "But first must get rid of Alexi car. Cannot leave here."

With Zim and Illiana in the Range Rover and Billy driving the mob car, they took another quick trip to the Marquette County Airport and stashed Alexi's Jaguar across the lot from Cully's Ford, then they hurried back to Loon Haven and spent the rest of the morning and all afternoon cruising every street within a ten-mile radius of town without seeing a trace of the Caddy. When dusk came, tired and hungry, they stopped at a pizzeria, bought two large pepperoni pizzas, and then drove home.

"We're screwed," whined Zim as they entered the kitchen. "We gotta get out of here. Let's just pack up and go."

Billy opened the top box and pulled out a slice, twirling a string of cheese on his finger. "I don't know, man. I like it here."

Zim's jaw dropped. "Just how long were you planning on staying?"

Billy shrugged. He hadn't thought it out.

"Is good pizza," said Illiana, using a napkin to wipe a dribble of oil from her chin.

"The best ones are greasy," said Billy. "I think they put olive oil on top."

Zim wolfed down a slice. "The sauce is zesty. I taste oregano and a pinch of cayenne."

"Garlic too," said Illiana, "and hint of fennel."

"Tangy and not too sweet," added Billy.

"New York Style," said Zim as he plowed into a second slice.

The phone rang and they stopped mid-bite. Illiana wiped her hands and picked up the receiver. "Vanko residence."

She listened. "Yes." Listened. "Fifty thousand, you say." Listened. "Mr. Vanko gone for day. I give message. You call back tomorrow noon." More listening. Her lips compressed. A reliable indication she was pissed. "You not hear good? I say call back tomorrow." Then she hung up.

"Smart-ass thief want fifty thousand to bring car back. He say if not pay, cops will find, and then trouble for Vanko. That mean trouble for us."

"A person can't even leave their car in their driveway anymore," said Billy, pulling another slice free. "What's this world coming to?"

"Morals declining," offered Illiana.

"From now on, I'm locking it in the garage."

"First, we gotta get it back," said Zim. "But we're dealing with a common criminal here, so we have the edge."

"How edge?"

"He's not a professional, at least not a professional blackmailer. He stole a car and found stiffs in the trunk, now the dingleberry thinks he's on easy street when actually he's screwed."

"How is screwed?"

"When you're a car thief and you got bodies rotting in the trunk of a hot Caddy and you're blackmailing the owner, what are you gonna do with the car?"

There were no takers.

"Well, you're not gonna park it on Main Street, that's for sure. You gotta hide it."

"So?" said Illiana.

"The longer you hide it, the worse the stink gets."

Zim tapped his nose. "And the stinkier the bodies get, the more he'll want to get rid of the car, but the harder that's going to be because by then it'll be stinking so bad that he won't want to get in and drive. See?"

Hands on her hips. "So?"

"That'll put pressure on him and force him to compromise, so that means we need to delay. Haggle about the price and haggle about where the drop will be and everything else. Every time he calls, tell him Vanko will let him know in the morning. That way the days will stretch on and on. And when all that's settled, tell him we need more time to get the money. Really drag it out. Make him sweat. But keep telling him we're going to pay. Then, after we hold him off as long as possible, set up a meet. He'll be desperate, but the last thing he'll want to do is to make the exchange in person. No one's that stupid. He'll come up with a plan to minimize his risk, and he'll want us to give him the money first. Needless to say, we can't do that, we'll just get a call later asking for more. We gotta make it so we meet face to face. Once that happens, bingo, problem solved."

Billy nodded. "Maybe we could have him pick up the money here. That'd be less work for everyone."

Zim began to say something but decided against it.

The night passed slowly and the next morning dragged. Then it was noon, and the trio sat anxiously in the kitchen awaiting the call.

The phone rang.

Illiana answered. "Vanko residence." She listened. "Mr. Vanko say fifty too much. He willing pay ten." She listened. "You not hear words from my mouth? Is not going to be fifty. Get that out of head. Mr. Vanko offer ten. You want make counteroffer? Make counteroffer. I tell. He is reasonable man." She listened. "Yes, I think twenty good counter. You call back ten minutes." She hung up.

"Jesus!" said Zim. "I don't never want to be hagglin' price with you."

Billy smiled. He was proud of her.

Exactly ten minutes later, the blackmailer called back.

"Mr. Vanko say sixteen is maximum." She listened. "Mr. Vanko did not like car. Mr. Vanko did not like people. Mr. Vanko say sixteen, take or leave." She listened. "That is good. You are thinking with head. All right. You bring car back and pick up money." She listened. "Is less work for everyone if you bring." She listened. "That is smart." She hung up.

"Well?" prodded Zim, uncomprehending.

"Thief will be here in twenty minutes."

Billy the Squid was already flexing his fingers.

# Fifteen

**After dispatching the** dumbest blackmailer in America, the trio set out with a carload of dead bodies, two rotting in the trunk and one seeping gas on the back seat. From a business perspective, it made sense dealing in volume; nevertheless, driving around in a corpse wagon gave Zim the willies. "How about the sewage treatment plant for a change?"

"Kinda public," replied Billy. "Probably people there."

"County dump?"

"Fine with me, but they'd get found."

"Forest," said Illiana. "Is more work but best for keep secret."

Zim groaned. Digging a hole large enough to hold three people was going to be hard work. He did not like hard work. "Isn't there someplace else? Something that doesn't involve so much digging?"

"Acid bath," said Illy.

"Yuck!"

"Lye pit."

"Don't know where one is."

"Wrecking yard with car squashing."

"Town's too small."

"Bury in concrete."

"Ain't seen no construction sites."

"Throw in mineshaft."

"Ain't seen none of them either."

"Tie weights to legs and sink in big lake."

"We'd need a boat."

"Only leaves forest," said Illiana. "Already have shovels."

Zim resigned himself to the labor.

A half-hour later found them twenty miles from the castle on scenic Forest Highway 13, searching for a quiet road to nowhere.

"There," said Zim, pointing to a two-rut trail leading into the woods.

Billy swung the Caddy off the highway.

"I see tire tracks," said Illiana. "Not private enough."

Zim rolled his eyes. "It'll be fine. Anyway, it's a road, there are bound to be tracks. Let's drive in and see."

They bounced along through sandy ruts for perhaps a quarter mile before the road ended at an idyllic ten-acre pond ringed by a narrow beach. There was an inviting grassy area near the shore shaded by a giant maple, its leaves a brilliant display of fall colors.

Billy braked to a stop where the grass met the sand. "Wish I had a pole." He'd never had a fishing pole.

There was a buttery sun in the sky and just enough breeze to coax the honey-hued leaves on the nearby birches to flutter.

"Good place for picnic," said Illiana. "Have plenty time. Maybe when done, go store, get food, come back."

Billy had never been on a picnic or gone fishing. They were just things he'd seen on TV in reform school or the joint or during the brief periods in between. Fun things that other people did. Normal people. Billy wanted to be normal too, and to take pleasure from these innocent activities. He nodded enthusiastically. "Let's do it, babe! It'll be fun." Bubbling with enthusiasm, he turned to Zim, "Come on, man. Let's go up the road a ways and toss the bodies. Illiana can take the Caddy and get food and stuff while we bury 'em. Then we can have a picnic. What do you say?"

It was the longest string of words Billy had ever put together. Zim was impressed. And notwithstanding his distaste for burying bodies, it seemed like a good idea. "Hmm . . . a couple six-packs and a fishing pole would suit me fine. Maybe some fried chicken and potato salad. Yeah, sure, count me in."

"Must do bodies first," said Illiana.

It made sense, so Billy turned the car around and drove back along the road, stopping at a random spot. "Good as any," he said, popping the trunk and climbing out of the car. Zim and Illy followed.

Behind the Caddy, the stench from the bodies was overwhelming. Zim covered his mouth with his hand and used his thumb and forefinger to pinch his nose.

Illiana said, "I walk up road. Make sure no surprise."

Zim gave an abbreviated nod.

"Let's do the gross ones first," said Billy, grinning.

Zim took a deep breath and reached for the ankles.

Twenty minutes later, exhausted and sweating from the effort, Billy and Zim had managed to carry all three stiffs a good two hundred feet into the woods. There they lay, side-by-side, in a small clearing suitable for digging.

Zim said, "Jesus! That's a lot of work. We gotta find a better way."

"All part of the job," said Billy. "We're professionals."

"Billy! Zim!" They turned and saw Illiana rushing toward them through the trees. "Car is coming!"

Billy had the Glock tucked in his waistband. He touched it for reassurance.

They heard the sound of a vehicle on the road and then the bleating of a horn.

Zim said, "Probably pissed 'cause the Caddy's blocking 'em. Billy, you'd best move it."

Illiana turned to Zim, "How about you stay. Guard bodies, rest, dig. Billy and I move car, get food, then come back. Not seem right two men and one woman walk out of woods."

She had a point. "Yeah, go. But hurry up. If the people in that car stick around, it could cause problems."

The horn sounded again.

"Hold on to your fucking shorts," yelled Zim. "I'm takin' a dump."

"Fuck you, asshole," came the reply. "Move your goddamned car or we'll ram it."

Zim's brow furrowed. Plans were out the window. "Gimme the Glock."

Billy complied, and with Zim in the lead, the trio marched out of the forest and up to the passenger side of a jacked up, camouflaged pickup outfitted with enough lights for a space ship. Two fleshy rednecks sat in the cab drinking beer, empty cans on the ground by to the door, rifles in a rack, tips of fishing poles hanging over the tailgate. Their windows were rolled down. As Zim approached, the nearest to him said, "Fuck you doin' parking in the middle of the road? City boy in your fag car, come up here and think you own it all. Get that pussy-mobile moved, asshole, or we'll push it out of the way."

"How 'bout you gum my wood?" replied Zim. It just came out. Now he was quoting dead mob women. Where would it end?

"Fuck you," said the one nearest to him, opening his door as a prelude to some asskicking.

Zim's eyes narrowed and his jaw tightened. Then he emptied the Glock into the cab with a gusto that surprised Illiana—her thinking he didn't have the guts for it.

After the last echo died away, Billy said, "Good work. Pricks deserved what they got." Then he walked over and buffed a dead moth off the grill of the Caddy. "Wanna keep it nice."

The rednecks were fat, and dragging their carcasses to the burial ground was difficult. When they were done, Zim was beat, slumping to the ground and lying next to the last stiff in a line of five.

"Must get rid of truck," said Illy.

"I'm tired," mumbled Zim.

"Zimmy, you stay here and relax. We'll take care of the truck and get some eats for a picnic."

Like a wedding at a funeral, he thought. Too weary to argue, "Yeah, sure. I'll wait."

Billy and Illy trod off. Soon he heard the vehicles start up and drive away. After that, the forest was quiet.

Lying on the soft grass, hands behind his head, Zim stared up at the sky. The temperature was in the low-eighties, a light breeze caressed his skin. Sunlight filtering through the leaves above created an ever-changing kaleidoscope of shapes and colors, soothing his mind and relaxing his body. Higher up, clouds drifted past. White cottony shapes on diaphanous strings. Snowy lambs against a soft blue background. There's one lamb, he thought. There's two. There's three. There's . . . zzzzzzz.

And Zim dreamed of lambs and blue sky. And he dreamed he was in was in his Godfather suit and he and Remy were cozying up at the bar. His dream segued to the castle. They were in bed, her next to him, close, kissing. He stroked her hair. He felt himself get hard. He wanted her, she was willing, he began to mount.

# Sixteen

**September is bird-hunting** season. When the hunter stumbled upon the scene, Zim, deep in REM sleep, was applying a slow but perceptible pelvic thrust to a fully clothed redneck with a half-dozen bullet holes in him. The hunter was not young. His heart was not good. Five dead bodies and a ghoul dry fucking one of them was too much. In shock, the shotgun slipped from his fingers. When it hit the ground, it fired. The birdshot blew off much of the rotting foot of Alexei Petrovich. The noise jarred Zim awake. The sight of the redneck startled him. He leaped to his feet. The hunter was ten feet away. He stared at Zim. Zim stared back. There was blood around his mouth from nuzzling in the vicinity of a bullet hole in the redneck's cheek. It looked as though he'd been feeding. The old hunter grabbed his chest, gasped for breath, fell to his knees. His last words before dying were, "Don't eat me!"

Zim was in shock. He staggered around the small

clearing on the beautiful fall day with the light breeze fluttering golden leaves trying to grasp what his life had become. He reflected on his self-image as a footloose iconoclast, breaking the rules as he saw fit and living life to the fullest—a moment-by-moment existence with no future and no past—and along with that, basically a good person, worthy of friendship and trust and respect. He realized it was difficult to reconcile involvement in a long string of murders with being a good person. The gardener and the cookie lady were the problems. All the others were assholes. Fuck 'em. Some people need killing. Nothing more than culling the herd to make the world a better place. But the gardener was different, doing his mostly thankless labor for bottom-end dollars and no status. Wife at home packs his lunch, makes his dinner, probably got kids and grandkids too. The guy deserved better. And the cookie lady, geez, why? Zim was sorry they'd killed them. It was the first thing he'd ever been sorry for in his entire life. It made him feel strange. It made him feel bad. He felt the same way about feeling bad as he did about work, he didn't like it. He knew he had to stop killing people. He really, really had to stop.

On strange impulse, or perhaps at this point purely from habit, he walked over to the old man, grabbed his ankles, and dragged him in line with the others. While doing so, he glanced down at his shirt. There were bloodstains on the flannel that mirrored the bullet holes in the redneck. He'd been on top of him for chrissake! No one must ever know. He *had* to wash the blood off or Billy and Illy would figure it out.

Zim dashed through the woods to the road and turned

right and sped to the pond. Standing on the shore, he took stock. There was blood on his shirt, pants, hands, and face. There was no alternative. He tested the water with a finger. It was cool but tolerable. He took a deep breath and then slowly stepped in. Then another step, then another, deeper and deeper until he was up to his chest. Gathering his courage, he bent his knees and went under, rubbing his face and clothing to wash off the blood. Coming up, he took a fresh breath and went under again, repeating the scrubbing procedure. The third time he came up, he had an audience.

"Zimmy! Gettin' down with a little swimming. All that digging make you hot?"

Zim sloshed out of the water.

"You always wear shoes when swim?" asked Illiana.

Zim stared down at his feet. "I forgot."

"The excitement of a beautiful day," said Billy, filled with bliss.

"Why you not with bodies?" asked Illiana.

"Ah, well, something came up."

"What? What come up?"

They slogged back to the clearing, and Zim showed them the hunter.

Billy said, "You're a bad dude, Zimmy. You just stare at a guy and he dies. Way to build a rep."

Zim didn't think it was so cool. Didn't want to think about it at all. And he really, really didn't want to see any more dead bodies. "Let's do it. I can't look at 'em anymore."

Illiana nodded. "Work ethic is improving."

It took nearly two hours to scour out a pit large enough to sleep six. A Herculean task. When the bodies were in and the last shovelful tossed on top, Zim's back and arms ached.

"Time to picnic," said Billy, then he raced through the woods to the pond where Illiana had spread a blanket to sit on and had cold beer in cans and foot-long submarine sandwiches at the ready—which was the best she could do under the circumstances—and, courtesy of the rednecks, two fishing poles leaned against the maple tree. When Billy saw it, he was ecstatic. "Oh, sweetie, that's nice."

"Is for you, Billy. Come and enjoy."

Illy and Billy ate and drank and then went skinny-dipping, giggling and splashing water at each other, swimming far out, kissing, and then swimming back in again. Zim sat on the shore in his soggy clothes gnawing on the end of a sub and slamming beer after beer until he passed out. As he was abandoning consciousness, he imagined he'd wake up in jail. Maybe it wouldn't be so bad, considering.

Just before sunset, Billy helped him to the car. When they arrived home, Zim was semi-conscious. "No," was all he said as they escorted him inside and put him to bed. Afterward, Illy and Billy drifted down to the kitchen.

"Zim was kind of freaked out," said Billy.

"Not have strong mind like you," replied Illiana. "Must separate business from personal life. Maintain balance."

Billy nodded, marveling at how smart she was.

Maintain balance, yeah, he guessed that's how he did it, didn't let business get in the way of the enjoyment of life. "Cocktails in the library?"

"Is excellent idea, lover boy, but first must change clothes."

Billy smiled. He'd wear his new tan slacks and Vanko's smoking jacket.

# Seventeen

The next morning Zim was more himself. The three were eating breakfast when Illy said, "Cops will come today about gardener."

Zim tensed. With so many bodies, he'd lost track of the specific legal and evidentiary issues associated with each one.

Billy nonchalantly devoured a slice of bacon. "Think so?"

She held up a business card with a blue shield. "Cop put in door. Not see last night. I find on porch this morning. Has note, want Vanko to call."

"What should we do?" asked Billy.

Zim's mind screamed *RUN!*

Illiana calmly set the card on the table and ran through the chronology. "Gardener not come home. Wife call police. Cop come that night. When get here, house dark, no one home. Cop come again yesterday. No one home. Leave card. If not call, will come today."

"Call 'em," said Zim, stating the obvious.

"Yes, is best. I will say gardener come, do work, leave bill, drive away, that all I know. Vanko on vacation for week. Not back one more. I am only one here. They want talk? No problem."

"But what if they wanna come and take a look?" asked Billy.

"Still not problem. You and Zim are hiding. I say Vanko gone. I alone. They want see, I show. Nothing to see, they go away."

"Zimmy, what say you and I drive back to the pond and hide out in the woods?"

Zim blanched. He imagined them in the forest, lost and wandering. Night would come. A rotting hand would push its way through moist earth. Then another. Then another. Soon they'd all be out. Clots of dirt and hunks of putrid flesh falling from their sightless bodies as they staggered forward, chasing him through the murky woods. Illiana's voice brought him back.

"Can do if want, but not necessary."

"But if the cops check the house, they'll find us," said Billy.

She shook her head. "Not find."

"No?"

"Is secret room."

Zim's mouth opened, but no sound came out.

Billy said, "Secret room? Cool! Show me."

The grim bookcase in Vanko's office was the entrance. Pressing a tiny spot on the paneling beneath the lowest shelf caused a four-foot section of bookcase to open like a door, books and all. Behind it was a small but comfortable room, six feet wide by ten feet long. At one end were shelves stocked with food, beverages, blankets and pillows, books and magazines, a television that could be switched between security cameras and cable, two pairs of headphones for listening, a telephone, and an arsenal of handguns. In the center of the room were two padded folding chairs and a small table. At the other end was a compact kitchen/bathroom combination with a curtain for privacy. The walls and ceiling were covered with buff-colored soundproofing, and the floor had thick buff carpeting laid over rubber matting to eliminate noise and provide a comfortable place to rest. Additionally, the walls, ceiling, and door were plated with half-inch steel, and the sub-floor was reinforced concrete. A dedicated air conditioning system provided comfort, and an array of locks assured no one would be entering without permission. Best of all, the architect had designed the room so that its space would not be missed. It was a fortress within a fortress.

"Wow!" said Billy, impressed.

"It's like a damn jail cell," said Zim. Backing away, stomach queasy.

"Better to sit in chair and read magazine one hour than sit in prison watch back fifty years."

"Lot better," chimed Billy, totally sold.

After turning off the lights and closing the door, Illiana said, "Bend down. I show how open. Is tricky."

Billy got down on his hands and knees, Zim only in a crouch. Illiana lay on the floor and pointed to a spot at the top right corner under the lowest bookshelf. "I find when cleaning. Must press special place then door open. Billy, you try."

Using his finger, Billy pushed where Illiana showed him. The door silently opened an inch. Illy pushed it closed. "Zim, now you try."

"I got it," said Zim, tired of being schooled on simple tasks.

Illiana rose to her feet. "Now must call cops."

"I gotta use the bathroom," said Zim.

"Not necessary to tell."

Billy and Illy were in the kitchen, Billy polishing off the rest of his breakfast and Illy composing herself for the phone call, but just as she was about to pick up the receiver, the phone rang.

"Vanko residence."

"This is Officer Hardwick of the Loon Haven Police Department. I'd like to speak to Mr. Vanko?"

"Mr. Vanko not home. Go on trip. I only one here."

"Are you a relative, ma'am?"

"I am maid."

"Mind if I ask you a couple of questions?"

"Not mind. You ask."

"I'm outside on my cell phone, mind if I come in?"

Illiana froze. "Is okay . . . I upstairs. Give time for come down open door."

Billy stopped eating when the phone rang. He sensed Illiana's discomfort as the conversation progressed. When the receiver was back in its cradle, he asked, "What's up, babe?"

Her tone was urgent. "Cop out front. Want come in.

Go safe room. I find Zim. When cop gone, I come tell."

Billy nodded and made a beeline to Vanko's office. He lay on the floor, pushed the secret spot, pulled the bookcase open, hurried inside, and pulled it closed behind him.

Illiana quickly tossed all but her own breakfast dishes in the dishwasher and then went searching for Zim. She didn't dare call his name for fear the cop might hear, so she raced upstairs to his bedroom and rapped on the bathroom door. "Zim! Cop here. Must go to safe room."

"What?"

She tried the handle. It was locked. She pounded. "Zim! Must come now! Cop here. Go safe room!"

Wearing nothing but his beehive underwear, he opened the door. "What?"

"Cop is here! Go safe room." She turned and ran for the front door.

The cop was big, six-four, two-sixty, wearing a neatly pressed uniform with a Loon Haven shield stitched to the pocket. He towered over skinny Illiana dressed in tank top, shorts, and bare feet. "I'm Officer Hardwick, ma'am."

Illiana stared up at him. "You want ask question?"

"Yes, ma'am." He glanced over her head, craning to see as much of the inside as possible.

"You want come in?"

"If you don't mind, ma'am."

"Not mind," she said, stepping out of the way. She didn't mind if he entered the foyer, but she wasn't going to allow him anywhere else without cause.

The cop stepped inside, glanced around. "Quite a place here."

"Yes. Is what Mr. Vanko like."

"And your name?"

"Illiana. I am maid."

"You say he's gone away?"

"Go on trip. Leave last week. Come back next."

"And you're the only one here?"

Illiana's lips pinched. "Have already said am only one. Why ask?"

"Just curious, ma'am."

"What you want?"

"It's about your gardener, Cully Hixon. He is your gardener, isn't he?"

"Cully Hixon is gardener, yes."

"Has he been here recently?"

"Was here two days ago. Did work. Left bill."

"Then what happened?"

"Happened?" She shrugged. "Went away. Come back next week."

"And he left a bill?"

Illiana's brow furrowed. "Is what I said. Why you ask everything twice?"

"Just trying to get it straight." He paused, then he tilted his head. "Could I see the bill?"

Billy had given it to her the day they dispatched Hixon. Out of habit, she'd placed it on Vanko's desk. "I will get." She turned and began walking toward the office. The cop followed her. She debated telling him to stay put but thought it might create more problems than it solved. Anyway, by this time Billy and Zim would be in the safe room, so it didn't matter.

After Illiana ran out of his room, Zim grabbed his clothes and blazed a trail to Vanko's office. He expected to see Billy standing there, door to the safe room open, but the bookcase was closed. Zim panicked and dove to the floor to find and press the secret button that would open the door. Head pressed to the carpet, his eyes scanned the area beneath the shelf for an obvious place to push. Seeing none, his fingers worked the wood like a lunatic accountant . . . but the door would not open. He could hear Illiana and the cop talking. *There were footsteps coming down the hall!* Desperate, Zim's eyes darted about for a place to hide. Other than two chairs and the bookcase, the only piece of furniture was Vanko's desk. He had no choice. Scurrying behind it, he bundled his clothes, hunched as low as possible, then ducked his head and waddled into the void where a person's legs would usually be. He was under the top, between the drawers, arms hugging his calves, head clamped between his knees. He could see light from the hallway shining on his toes.

As Illiana entered the office, the first things she saw were Zim's feet under the desk. *Is idiot!* she thought. Then her arm shot up, finger pointing to the weaponry on the walls as the cop entered the room. "Mr. Vanko, is collector."

The cop's eyes followed hers to the bloody hatchet. "Weird."

"Yes," agreed Illiana. "Mr. Vanko is odd man but okay. Pay good. Treat right. No problem."

She kept his gaze fixed on the wall as they crossed the room. Arriving at the desk, Illiana stepped behind it. The gardener's bill was lying where she'd left it. She picked it up and held it out in a way that drew the cop to the side of the desk, not in front where he might see Zim. While he was studying the bill, she imagined chaining Zim in a dungeon and doing unspeakable things to him with a red-hot poker. It gave her some relief. She smiled.

The cop said, "Mind if I take this with me?"

"Not mind. Just tell total so Mr. Vanko can pay when get back."

"Three hundred and forty dollars."

Illiana nodded. "Gardener is missing?"

The cop stiffened. "Who said anything about missing?"

Illiana's face transformed into a picture of innocence. "You ask about gardener. Why ask if not missing?"

The cop nodded. "Yeah, you're right. Disappeared the day he did your lawn. Didn't make his later appointments and never got home. Trying to figure out what happened between here and his next stop."

"Two days. Not good."

The cop nodded. "You saw him when he was here?"

"Yes, when bring bill to door."

"Was there anything unusual about him? Did he seem nervous or upset? Anything like that?"

She paused to ponder the question then shook her head. "Not unusual. Same as always."

The cop nodded. "Well, thank you for your cooperation, Illiana. If I have more questions, do you mind if I call?"

"Not mind. Glad to help." She gave him a smile to demonstrate sincerity.

He smiled back. "I can find my way out."

As the cop turned and strode for the door, Illiana relaxed and sat down in the high-backed chair behind Vanko's desk. As soon as she did, she realized her mistake . . . but it was too late. The cop would turn back at the door for a parting word. He would see Zim's feet. There was no time to hustle around the desk to block his view, so she pulled the chair up to the desk and shoved her legs into what little space remained in the void. In the process, a sharp toenail caught Zim in a particularly tender spot under the armpit and the pain caused his head to jerk upward, striking the bottom of the desk drawer with a loud *whack!* In anger, Illiana dug the nail in deeper. Zim's eyes began to water. He imagined imprisoning her in a dungeon and doing terrible things to her with a red-hot poker. The cop was at the door on his way out. Hearing the noise, he stopped and turned. Illiana gave him her warmest smile. Zim toes dug into the carpet in response to the pain. The cop saw the movement under the desk and stared. The woman had some darn big feet. Hairy, too. He glanced up at her slender body and then down again at the feet. Must be a European thing. Probably from crossbreeding with Neanderthals . . . or Hobbits. Damned glad he'd married local. Couldn't imagine having those furry dogs tickling his shins all night and flapping around like swim fins on the bedroom floor every morning. "Have a nice day, ma'am." He saw the toes wiggle. Jesus, they were huge! Poor girl. He bit his lip and walked out.

As soon as she heard the front door close, Illiana pulled her legs free and rushed to the front of the house, peering through a window to make sure the cop was leaving. After his cruiser disappeared up the driveway, she gave a sigh of relief then marched back to the office. Zim was still under the desk. She ignored him and opened the bookcase. Billy was relaxing in one of the chairs. He smiled when he saw her.

"Is okay. Cop gone."

"Any problems?"

"No, but will come back. Not give up so easy."

Hearing the conversation, Zim eased himself from beneath the desk and stood up, working out kinks as he did. "Just how long were you going to leave me under there?"

Illiana went full boil. "Why you not go in safe room? Why hide under desk like insect?"

"Didn't have time," he whined, unwilling to admit he couldn't find the latch.

"Almost get us caught. I am thinking you not know how open bookcase."

"I do so."

Her hands went to her hips. "Show."

Billy closed the bookcase. Zim procrastinated. Illy tapped her foot.

"Oh, all right." Zim proceeded to the bookcase and got down on the floor then poked at every square centimeter under the shelf but, needless to say, the door did not open. Illiana's eyes went to the ceiling and she growled in exasperation. Peacemaker by default, Billy got down next to Zim and showed him where to press. Zim pressed. The door opened.

# Eighteen

"**W**e gotta go," said Zim. "We gotta go now! You said it yourself, Illiana, the cops will be back. We could be sitting here in the kitchen talking or eating or whatever, and they could stroll around and see us through the window and start blasting. To be anywhere near safe, we'd have to spend every second of every day in the safe room."

"Safe room," repeated Billy, thinking staying there would be like camping or a sleepover, things he'd never done but wouldn't mind trying.

Zim made a sour face. "It'd be like jail. Or worse, the hole. I can't handle tight spaces. I need elbowroom. I'll take my chances on the run. You two oughta come with me. What do you say?"

"I cannot go," replied Illiana. Billy gazed at her, uncomprehending. "Told cop I am maid. Said okay ask more questions. Cannot leave or cop get suspicious. Must stay."

Zim was desperate. "You and I, Billy Boy, come on, let's hit the road."

Billy shook his head. "I like it here. I want to stay." Illiana was next to him. He put his arm around her and gave her a hug.

Zim opened his mouth to argue but stopped. "All right. Fucking crazy, but if you two wanna stay, do it. I'm getting out."

Illiana was all for it. "Take Cadillac. Leave in lot at Green Bay bus station."

"The Caddy?" said Billy, disappointed.

"Is better, Billy. Had bodies inside. If cops bring dogs, they smell, then problems."

Billy frowned. "I love that car."

"We will get another," she consoled.

"Why do I have to drive the stinkmobile?" complained Zim. "Why do I have to take all the risk?"

"Already said. Cannot have car here. Too dangerous. Is only three-hour drive Green Bay. No risk if careful. Once car in lot, no problem. Mail ticket and key. After heat off, Billy and I will get. Make clean. Sell and buy new."

Billy smiled. He was all for a new Caddy.

"I'm gonna load up and go," said Zim, his resolve buttressed by fear.

"Not load. No time sell things. Take money. Drive Green Bay. Take bus Minnesota. Stay with friends. Keep mouth shut. When Billy and I get money, we will come and share. If want, all go Argentina. You write address where we can find."

"Fine," said Zim, and did what he was told.

After going upstairs to grab his suitcase, he came down to the kitchen to say his goodbyes. "We got history together, Billy Boy. Don't forget about me."

"I won't, Zimmy." Billy stepped forward and gave him a hug. Zim thought it was embarrassing but hugged him back.

When the embrace ended, Zim's eyes went to Illiana.

"Not necessary," she said. "Necessary drive safe, get on bus, go Minnesota. Not tell friends about money or they take. Not tell about castle or they come. Not tell about crimes or they blackmail. Understand?"

At the end of his rope, Zim replied, "Anything else? Number of farts? Times I take a leak?"

She frowned. "Not need be mean. Am just trying keep safe." Billy's face wrinkled in disdain at Zim's attitude. Illy saw it. Checkmate. In only a few minutes, Zim would be gone, hopefully forever, and she and Billy would be infinitely safer.

Her life had been so chaotic over the past two weeks that Illiana had not thought deeply about her future, for the most part reasoning that with Zim under control, or better yet gone, the situation was manageable. But then came the gardener incident. He was their most pressing problem. And eventually Remy Torriano would be missed. The combination would be too much to handle. Too many commonalities. Too many fingers pointing at the castle and its residents. Too many questions. The police would insist on talking to Vanko in person. Zim, assuming he didn't sweat himself into a quivering puddle of goo, would never pass. And when Vanko failed to make contact, the police would come with more questions. When

Hardwick was here, she told him that she'd taken the bill from the gardener, and when Remy Torriano is missed, investigators will find she was at the Woodland Inn with Zim. It's not as though anyone would forget him in his Godfather suit, or Billy knocking out Remy's boyfriend, or her cajoling the crowd back to life. The police would come. They'd insist on seeing identification. Afterward, they'd know who she was. And then, if she were to slip away, they'd have her name and history and everything needed to track her down. And they would ask pointed questions about the night at the Woodland Inn and about the people she was with. She'd be forced to construct fantastic lies to explain everything and then repeat those lies over and over under withering scrutiny. She knew she was strong, but she wasn't sure she was that strong. Zim was right. They should leave now. But not together. Let Zim go on his way. She and Billy would be safer without him.

"See ya," said Zim. He grabbed the car keys from the counter and turned away and strolled through the house, out of the front door, and straight to the garage. Tossing his suitcase in the back seat, he climbed in the driver's side, keyed the ignition, punched the remote, and watched in the rearview mirror as the garage door slid up. When the door motor stopped whining, he craned his neck around and began to back out. He'd barely begun when he spied the nose of a black limo creeping up the drive and panicked. *The mob! I gotta get outta here!* Zim jammed his foot on the gas, and the engine roared. His body was turned to the right, head twisted to look behind him, left hand pulling down on the steering wheel for support. When he punched the gas, the tires squawked and the Caddy lurched backward, nose veering to the right, and crashed into the side of the doorway with a horrific crunching and scraping. Panic stricken, he stomped on the accelerator. The wheels spun furiously, emitting an air-raid siren scream as black smoke billowed from the wheel wells, but the car did not budge.

The mob car was at the circle drive. A gurgling sound came from Zim's throat. He yanked his foot off the gas, dropped the gearshift into drive, and with a shriek of metal, pulled the car forward so that it was completely in the garage. Then he jabbed at the remote until the door closed.

Like a child hiding from a monster, Zim desperately wanted to stay in the Caddy and pretend he was invisible, but he knew he had to get back in the castle. There were guns inside. They could hold them off.

Leaping from the vehicle, he dashed through the garage and flew out the side door, racing to the entrance of the house just as the limo was pulling up to the steps. Without so much as a glance at the car or its occupants, he opened the front door, zipped inside, and slammed it shut behind him, quickly locking all three deadbolts. The noise brought Illy and Billy from the kitchen. Illiana read the terror on his face. "What is problem?"

*"It's the mob!"* he stuttered. *"They're outside!"*

Her brow furrowed, and she hurried to the peephole. Looking through it, her body tensed. Turning to Billy and Zim, she said, "Is bad."

# Nineteen

**Zim's eyes closed** in despair. "We're dead."

"Don't be idiot," said Illiana. "Not dead till dead."

"Distinction without a difference," he moaned.

"Is Nadia Nublinska and bodyguards. Dangerous, but can handle."

Billy had already dashed back to the kitchen and fetched the Glock. He stood in the center of the foyer, gun in hand, strangely at ease, a man defending his home. "Zimmy, buck up, dude. This is our crib. Ain't no fuck-nuts mob punks gonna muscle us out." He turned to Illiana. "Want me to shoot 'em?"

There was a loud *rap, rap, rap* as the knocker struck the door. Illiana grimaced. "Not necessary . . . yet, but must be careful. She stared at Zim. "Go hide in safe room." He gave a quick nod and streaked toward Vanko's office. "Billy, put on sport coat. Keep gun hidden." She patted the small of her back. Billy nodded and headed for the staircase. Once he was out of sight, Illiana sighed and straightened herself, then unlocked the deadbolts and opened the door.

The woman standing before her wore a tawny sweater made of threads that shimmered when she moved, and vanilla stretch pants that mapped every fascinating curve. Her blonde hair was lit from within and flowed in a golden mane to her pendent breasts. Nordic genes on loan from Stockholm to Saint Petersburg had blessed her with an elegant face, hypnotic eyes, an alluring smile, and a body that made men drool. Even to Illiana, who wasn't inclined to swing both ways, she was astonishingly sexy. Yes, Nadia Nublinska, Alexei Petrovich's girlfriend, was a dangerous woman indeed. Best get rid of her fast.

Illiana affected a warm smile. "Nadia! Is good to see you."

The blonde gazed at her in sympathy. "Illiana. Is surprise. When I hear Alexei sell you, I feel sad. Thought maybe cheap sex work."

The insult made Illiana cringe.

"Later, I find he give you to Vanko for house drudge." She shrugged. "Not so bad, eh?"

Illiana's smile stayed firm. "What bring you?" She saw Nadia glance over her shoulder and knew Billy was back.

"Where are manners, Illiana? You not invite in and introduce to handsome man?"

Billy was stunned at her beauty. Stunned as well that she'd want to meet him.

Dangerous like poisonous snake, thought Illiana. "Of course. Rude of me. Come in." She stepped back and opened the door wide.

Nadia walked into the foyer, hips in motion, each step worthy of a full-length documentary. Her eyes were locked on Billy's. His eyes were locked on hers. Looking away was not possible. She went directly to him and gazed at him as if he were a deity. Her hand rose, soft fingers brushing his cheek and touching his lips. She turned to gauge Illiana's reaction, then a catty smile appeared. "Illiana, I would not have expected." Her smile widened.

Two goons lumbered in, stocky Slavic men with thick necks and a genetic predisposition toward violence. Illiana turned her attention to them. "Mr. Vanko say no guns in house. Must give to Billy." She gestured to him. Neither made any attempt to comply. "Nadia, tell them."

"I cannot," she said breezily. "Alexei would not allow. Where is he?"

"Alexei and Oz leave yesterday."

Surprise took Nadia. "Cannot be. He say he come see Vanko. Tell me to meet here. Afterward, go vacation to Canada."

Illiana shrugged. "Did not mention."

"Where is Vanko?"

"Vanko and wife go Detroit. I am only one here."

"Not only one," said Nadia with the rise of an eyebrow.

"Billy is Vanko's man."

"Not your man?"

It was difficult to say, but she had to. "No."

"Is good, Illiana." Nadia was still standing in front of Billy. She placed a hand on his bicep, felt it harden. Gazing at Billy but speaking to Illiana, "Maybe I use for pleasure before ride home."

I never want to leave here, thought Billy. Never, never, never.

With Billy stunned and out of commission, Illiana gave up on disarming the bodyguards. "Long drive. You want eat?" She led the group into the kitchen.

Zim was in the safe room monitoring live video of the mob woman via closed-circuit television. There was conversation taking place. He donned on a pair of headphones and twisted some knobs but couldn't get any audio, so he watched in envy as the Scandinavian babe sashayed across the foyer and toyed with Billy. Then, after the thugs came in, he followed the group across a split-screen as they moved into the kitchen.

Zim had been in the safe room for less than two minutes, and already he was sweating and claustrophobic. He hated the safe room. It felt as if the walls were closing in and he was suffocating. Mouth dry, head spinning, trapped like a rat in a stinking cage. How long could he last? A few days, a week maybe, then he'd have to come out. If he was lucky, they'd just shoot him. Maybe it wouldn't be so bad, considering. Overcome by vertigo, he lunged toward the sink for a glass of water, taking two quick steps before the headphone cord pulled tight and yanked the TV off the shelf.

"You want sandwich? I make."

Nadia glanced at Billy. "I know what I want, but will have to wait. Yes, Illiana, make sandwich. And bring glass of water, I am thirsty."

Illiana gritted her teeth and began to comply, but just

at that moment one of the thugs grunted, "I heard something," and pulled his gun. Billy came out of his trance and pulled his in response. The second thug saw him and pulled his, eyes locked on Billy. Billy sensed threat and shot him in the chest. Realizing there was no alternative, he shot the other thug too. "That takes care of that," he said, tucking the Glock back under his belt.

Nadia's eyes were wide. "Should not have done. Alexei will be angry."

"Own fault," said Illiana. "Should not have brought guns in house. Billy only do what Vanko tell him."

Nadia gazed at Billy, mind sifting through possibilities. "Thought just house boy, Illiana. Did not know was tough gangster."

Billy was flattered, but he knew there'd be trouble if he smiled.

"You must be one Alexei hear about."

Billy didn't speak.

"Billy the Squid."

He said nothing.

"Top professional choker."

He couldn't stand it and smiled a yes.

Illiana had had enough. "Maybe I have Billy show you?"

Billy hoped she wasn't serious. He couldn't imagine strangling Nadia Nublinska.

Right at that time, Zim came striding into the room. When Illiana saw him, her face fell. He'd watched Billy dispatch the thugs on closed circuit while putting the TV back on the shelf, and the mob woman was too enticing not to experience in person.

"Yo! What's up?" he said grinning, eyes glued to Nadia's cleavage and completely oblivious to the two bodies releasing fluids on the floor.

"Why not stay in room?" chided Illiana.

Zim ignored her. "And who do we have here?" he asked, sliding into a chair across the table from Nadia.

Nadia produced her most seductive smile. In a voice breathy with desire, "Illiana, shame on you. Why not tell have *two* handsome men keeping busy?"

Overcome by Nadia's goddess-like beauty and weapons-grade pheromones, Zim already had a hard on the size of a construction crane and was ready to kill to mate.

Billy was pissed at the inference that Illy would consider rubbing skin with Zim. Nadia had lost him. He glanced at Illiana. "What do you want me to do, hon?"

"We will see," she answered, relieved to be back in control. She directed her next statement to Nadia. "Is problem."

Nadia raised an eyebrow. "Yes?"

"You should not have come."

"Alexei said."

"Not matter what scum say."

"Illiana," her tone chiding, "is no way to talk about loving cousin. He care about you."

Illiana gave a half laugh. "Alexei Petrovich not care about anyone but self."

"Don't care 'bout nothin' now," said Billy.

Nadia Nublinska froze, but only for an instant, then she recalculated and moved forward. Reaching across the table, she took Zim's hand and stroked his palm. Instantly, a near-lethal charge of endorphins surged up his arm, through his neck, and into his brain, disabling it. "Who is handsome man?" she asked, her voice a silky purr, gossamer threads of desire drawing him closer.

Zim realized he'd forgotten his name. He struggled. Blurt out, "Zimdrek." Seemed right. Least close. He could have it legally changed.

She said the name. "Zimdrek." Each syllable a delectable confection of creamy-hot need. She leaned toward him. Her breasts rose and fell like swells in the ocean, his head moved up and down in response. Her eyes fixed on his. She whispered, "You are master."

Zim's mind was a rain-slicked road, steaming-hot day, twenty-car pileup, flaming gasoline tanker bearing down on him. A bead of sweat rolled off his forehead into his eye. He blinked it away. The master, yes, that's who I am. The brains. The boss. The head of this outfit. The Godfather. His suit was upstairs. Should he run up and put it on?

She said, "I am Nadia, and I have been longing to meet you."

"Me too," said Zim.

She made a sorrowful face. "Last man was bad to me. If you were my man, you would not be bad, would you?"

His head gyrated like a dog tearing up a toy.

She moved closer, tongue moistening lips the color of ripe cherries. "But maybe a little bad sometimes . . . yes?"

She stroked his arm and he gave a jerky nod. A little bad is good. Everybody likes a little bad. Some bad. Not much. Just a little. Just like she said. "I like a little bad," he agreed, voice cracking like a teenager. "Do you?"

Her body was in constant motion, swaying, teasing,

inviting. "With man like you . . . *anything.*"

For Zim, the word *anything* caused stars to collide and universes to explode. Something more extravagant than his wildest dream was unfolding. His brain screamed, *"Say something! Do something!"* but he was paralyzed.

Nadia moved closer yet, the scent of her perfume an ethereal drug lifting him to a higher plane. She gazed at him with the wanton lust of a love-starved slave woman. "I need man for physical pleasure. Man like you. Long ride. Must have now." Her free hand slid under the table to Zim's thigh. He panicked! He imagined hitting his thumb with a hammer. He imagined hitting his face with a hammer.

She whispered, "I need you inside."

Zim's head blew up, rubbery parts bouncing off the walls and zinging around the kitchen. Then, as if by magic, they all sprang back and reassembled themselves on his neck. Thinking he may have had a stroke, yet aching to lead his über-angel of sexual gratification up the gilded staircase to the land of nuclear orgasm, Zim gave a quick nod and rose, tipping his chair in the process. He held his hand out, bidding her to come.

"Whoring not work here," said Illiana.

"It'll work," said Zim.

"She not care about you. Use sex for control."

"Fine by me."

Illiana turned to Billy. "Shoot her."

Billy reached for the Glock.

Zim's eyes went wide. *"NO!"* he screamed, grabbing Nadia by the hand and pulling her behind him.

Nadia wrapped her arms tightly around Zim, her body

pressed against his, eyes on Illiana. "Alexei not satisfy me. I have been looking for real man." She pursed her lips and blew a thin stream of scented breath across Zim's ear and then used her tongue to flick the lobe.

For safety reasons, Zim backed the two of them out of the room and quickly dragged Nadia up the staircase to his lair.

After they were gone, Billy said, "That was weird," and opened the fridge in search of a snack.

Illiana was in awe of his ability to compartmentalize. "Woman is dangerous. No loyalty except to self. Boyfriend die, not shed tear, move on to next."

Billy nodded, checking out a package of salami.

"Now she have control of Zim."

"I'll say," responded Billy, there was pepperoni too. Maybe both would be good in a sandwich.

"Then she come after you."

"Don't have to worry about that, babe. You're my girl." Salami and pepperoni together with mustard and a piece of lettuce.

Illiana knew better. "Must kill."

That got Billy's attention. He closed the refrigerator. "Geez, hon. I don't know if I can do it."

She'd assumed as much. "I will do. Give gun."

Billy sighed and handed her the pistol. What a waste, he thought, then turned back to the refrigerator.

# Twenty

Illiana clicked the safety off on the Glock and marched out of the kitchen, climbed the stairs, and quietly tread the hall to Zim's room. Standing next to the door, she could hear the moaning and slapping of flesh that told her the rodeo had begun. She heard Zim say, "That's good. Yes! More!" She turned the knob and opened the door a crack. They were naked, clothes strewn about the floor, Zim lying on his back on the bed, eyes closed, teeth clenched in ecstasy. Nadia Nublinska's perfect body was on top, riding him like a horse, ass rising and falling in a steady rhythm, breasts bouncing, face toward the ceiling in fake bliss, golden hair splayed across her back swaying with each movement. Zim's hands were on her hips, directing her, forcing her down tight with each gallop. Moments later his arms reached out and pulled her torso to him, he arched his pelvis, pressing in, groaning with pleasure, then he collapsed, muscles slack, eyes closed in the drowsy sex haze of the afterward.

Illiana watched as Nadia decoupled. She whispered something into Zim's ear that made him smile, stroked his face, and then climbed off the bed in the direction of the bathroom.

There would never be a better time. Illiana rushed into the room, ran up behind Nadia, aimed the gun at her head, and pulled the trigger. There was a loud bang, and blood splattered against the wall.

Zim's body jackknifed into a sitting position. He gaped first at Illiana and then down at the formerly flawless body of his Russian sex goddess splayed across the floor. A tremulous *"no"* squeaked from his lips. Then his hands grabbed a pillow and he clutched it to his chest as his body convulsed in choking sobs.

Without a word, Illiana turned and walked out of the room.


"Heard the shot," said Billy, munching the last of his sandwich. "You gotta try it. Salami and pepperoni together. Really good."

"What kind of bread?"

"Seven grain. It's healthy."

"I like toasted."

Billy nodded approval. "I'll make you one."

She flicked the safety on and handed the gun to him. "Zim upset, but had to do."

"Your call, babe."

"Nadia too dangerous to keep as sex pet. I know her well. She is black widow spider. Take one hour, maximum, make Zim mindless robot. Afterward, she tell him kill, he not think different. Walk downstairs with smile on face, shoot us in head, walk back up for reward. Later, he asleep, she kill him too."

"Gotta do what you gotta do."

Illiana nodded. "But now have problem with Zim. Must get dressed and on road Green Bay. Otherwise, angry, cause problem. Plus, must get rid of bodies."

Billy gestured toward the dead thugs lying on the floor. "Dudes are big. Heavy, too. Had to shove one out of the way so I could open the fridge. Probably gonna need Zim's help loading 'em."

Illiana figured as much. "Is true. That mean must calm Zim. Help get through disappointing time."

Billy agreed and they marched upstairs to his room. They knocked. He didn't answer. They opened the door and gazed in. Zim was still naked on the bed, lying in a fetal position, arms wrapped tightly around his pillow, face buried in it.

Illiana softly inquired, "Zim?"

"What?" came the muffled response.

"Sorry, Zim. Had to do."

"No, you didn't."

"Did," said Illiana. "You not know her. She would control you. Then she kill you. No chance to live unless we kill."

"You did it because you can't stand to see me happy."

"Not true. I did to protect. You and us."

Zim sat up. "You probably killed Remy too!"

Billy looked away. Illy remained mute.

Zim's mouth opened in shock. "You did! You killed Remy, didn't you?"

Billy made a helpless gesture.

Illy said, "All in past. Not important. What important is drive Green Bay, take bus, see friends."

"No," said Zim, obstinate.

"Yes," said Illiana. "Must go. Take Cadillac. Be in Minnesota before night. Safe there. Find new woman."

"I don't want a new woman," he whimpered. "I want Nadia . . . or Remy."

"It's over," said Billy sympathetically. "What's done is done. Gotta move on. Plus, I need help loading the bodies."

Zim groaned and flopped back down. Pulling the pillow to his chest, he buried his face in it.

Billy turned to Illiana, "He'll be all right in a minute." Then to Zim, "Hey, bro, come on down when you're ready. I'll make you a really good sandwich."

"Sandwich?" he mumbled.

"Salami and pepperoni on seven-grain bread."

"You want mustard or mayonnaise?" asked Illiana.

Zim thought for a moment. "Mustard."

Billy said, "It'll be ready when you come down."

He wasn't right with it. Wasn't right with it at all. Why? Why *his* woman? Why not Illiana? But he knew why. Illiana had Billy by the short hairs, and he'd do whatever she told him. "It's good," he said, wiping a stray dab of mustard from his cheek.

Billy was sitting across from him at the kitchen table, Illiana to his left. He said, "When you're done, we should do the bodies."

Zim gave a fake shiver. "I'll help you load 'em, but that's it. Then I'm taking the Rover and I'm gone."

Illiana's brow furrowed. "Rover? Why Rover? Must take Cadillac."

"Can't, it's messed up. Something went wrong with the steering and it crashed against a wall. I gotta take the Rover."

Illiana's eyes doubled in size, forcing Zim to send his own on an inspection tour of the ceiling. "What car Billy and I use? Cannot stay forever. Too many people come. Cops for gardener and cowgirl. Mob for Alexei and Nadia. Alexei not so much, probably glad is gone. Not so Nadia. She hot property. Also, third cousin Gregor Bulnik. Him high up mobster. Smart, tough, mean. Third cousin go missing, cannot ignore. Must find those who take. Must punish. Not do, rivals think weak, challenge for turf, bad for cash flow. Gregor's men will ask questions. Get answers. Will come. No way to fool. Must leave."

Billy said, "There's that Ford pickup with the plow in the garage. It's in decent shape. I can take the plow off and we'll be fine. Let him take the Rover." He stood up and walked to the kitchen windows and then gazed out over the stonework to the English garden. He loved the garden, the scent of the flowers, the beauty and the peace. He turned back to Illiana. "I don't want to go."

She rose from the table and went to him. "Billy, but we must. Life is long. Do not worry, we will have like this again."

He shook his head. "It won't be the same."

"But cops will come and arrest. Or worse, mob will come and kill! No time, Billy. Will happen soon. Please, must go."

He shook his head again. His mind was made up. Whatever life he had left, he would live in his castle. He was Billy the Squid and this was his home and if anybody didn't like it, he'd kill 'em.

Zim was on his feet. "Billy Boy, you gotta listen to her. She's right, it's not going to work. Bad shit's comin' down if you stay. C'mon, Billy. Damn, man, you're the only friend I got. I don't wanna see you die. What do you say, bro? The three of us head out now in the Rover. Road trip, just like old times."

"Zim is speaking truth, Billy. Please, you must come with."

Billy smiled. "You two go on ahead, maybe I'll meet up with you in Minnesota."

"Will be too late," said Illiana in anguish. "Billy, please! I not want leave you, but I cannot stay. I not want die so young, not want rot in prison. We have time, Billy. Come, you will see. We will have more of good things. You and me, lover boy, together."

Billy smiled and shook his head one last time, then he asked, "You guys want some sandwiches for the road? I can do up a couple with salami and pepperoni?"

Illiana moved close and gave him a kiss. "I will miss you, Billy."

"I'll miss you, too. Stop by and visit when you can."

She was stunned by his naivety. Sooner or later, an hour, a day, a week, no longer, they would come. He wouldn't stand a chance against Gregor's men, and when the cops came, they'd be suspicious and insist on seeing ID. She knew he didn't have any, other than his own, and he couldn't show that. It just wouldn't work.

There was a tear in the corner of her eye. She wiped it away. "Goodbye, Billy."

"Don't you want to wait for the sandwich?"

She shook her head. "Zim and I must go. I will come back soon and visit. Then we will have bed fun, yes?"

Billy smiled.

# Twenty-one

**Z**im and Illiana were gone, the two arguing like a married couple all the way to the garage. Made Billy laugh. He watched from the steps as the Rover rolled up the driveway and out of sight and then went back into the kitchen and made himself another sandwich. Salami and pepperoni, mustard and lettuce, seven-grain bread. He took it into the library and set it on the coffee table in front of the leather couch. Then he fixed himself a drink. Cognac, neat. As he sat there sipping brandy and eating his sandwich, he thought about Zim and Illiana. He wished they hadn't left. He'd miss them. Illiana in particular. They'd had fun. Good, clean fun. Like the picnic and swimming in the pond. Then he thought of something else. Salami and pepperoni taste good.

# Twenty-two

Illiana was right, but not about the cops or mob. She was right about no one ever coming to the castle. Made Billy laugh. The days went by and no one came. Not the cops. Not the mob. Not anybody. He kind of wondered why. He'd prepared for the mob by stashing weapons from Vanko's arsenal in various places around the house and grounds so as to be ready for action. But they never showed. In the end, he guessed no one cared about Alexei Petrovich or Nadia Nublinska, least not enough to drive all the way up from Chicago. And the cops never came back asking about the gardener. He didn't know why, but figured they were busy with other things. He was sorry about the gardener. Sorry about the cookie lady too. And he vowed that in the future he'd only kill people who needed killing, like Rail's asshole boyfriend, Crowbar. After all, he was Billy the Squid, a respected professional. He had standards.

Billy decided not to hire a new gardener. He enjoyed

being outside and doing the work himself. It was man's work, and it made him feel good. And the lawn and garden never looked better.

No new murder-for-hire jobs came in. Billy assumed it was a marketing problem, but he had no idea of how to solve it. It didn't worry him though, he had money, his portion of the murder proceeds, and if push came to shove, there was plenty of stuff to sell. He'd be fine. Life was good. He was in his castle, the king of the castle, but the queen was gone and the jester too. He missed them, and he began to wonder if he'd made a mistake. The castle was grand, but it wasn't fun. People made it fun. People were important. It was an odd concept, and one he hadn't previously considered. He wondered if Illiana and Zim were more important than the castle. A strange concept indeed. He ruminated on these and other things as he went about his days, tending to the yard and garden and keeping up the house.

It was a cool afternoon in early October, sunny but with a wind from the northwest that promised rain. Shorter days had transformed the maples and birches into a brilliant sea of red, orange and yellow, swelling and waving with the breeze, leaves fluttering down, the landscape a shimmering panorama. It was two weeks to the day since Illiana and Zim had gone. Billy was in the front yard pruning roses when he heard a car on Chipmunk Lane. It slowed. It turned into the drive. Mob or cops, there was no one else. Dropping his shears, he sprinted along the edge of the yard to the back of the house, hurried inside, and retrieved the Glock from a drawer in the kitchen. Then he dashed to the front door, set the bolts, and ran back through the foyer to the hall, turned right and raced to the end room where he could watch the front of the house without being seen. Pressing his face to a window, he peered at a difficult angle toward the front yard. The glass distorted the view, but Billy could see the outline of a blue van parked by the entrance. There was an old woman in a long black dress with a shawl over her head standing by an open cargo door. She pushed a button and a pneumatic lift slid from beneath the van, rising to the level of the doorway. The woman climbed inside, and soon a wheelchair-bound figure appeared on the ramp. The man in the chair was old and hunched. A black watch cap covered his head, a thick plaid blanket was tucked around him for warmth. Vanko! thought Billy. But that didn't make sense.

The ramp descended to ground level. The woman pushed the wheelchair onto the pavement. Moving to the front, she bent low and spoke to the invalid, taking his hand to reassure him. Quivering, he jerked it away then wrapped his arms around himself in a piteous hug. The woman hung her head in despair. Then she rose and made her way toward the door.

Billy stood at the window, frozen. What should he do? He wished Illiana or Zim were around to help with the thinking. It was really hard. He couldn't decide, so he thought it best to pretend no one was home.

*Rap, rap, rap!* went the doorknocker. Just ignore it, he thought. They'll go away and everything will be fine. *Rap, rap, rap!* Billy put his hands over his ears. *Rap, rap, rap!* He didn't want to listen. All of a sudden, the rapping became urgent. *RAP! RAP! RAP! RAP! RAP!* He opened his eyes and glanced out the window. There was a second vehicle parked behind the first, a black limo like the one Nadia had arrived in. Large men with unfriendly faces were climbing out of it. *RAP! RAP! RAP! RAP! RAP!* Several had handguns, one a sawed-off shotgun. Fucking mob, thought Billy. It pissed him off. He watched the leader stride toward the front door until the window frame got in the way and he lost sight. Seconds later, the mob guy was back in view, dragging the woman behind him. Billy saw him ask her something. He saw spit fly out of her mouth onto his face. A hard left sent her reeling toward the house. The shawl fell away. She landed on the grass next to the steps and didn't move. Her face was in Billy's direction. His expression opened in realization. *It's Illiana!* Then he scowled. "Ain't no fucknuts mob punk gonna slap my girl."

Hand squeezing the Glock, he marched out of the room and down the hallway to the foyer. Unlocking the door, he swung it wide, brought up the gun, and drilled two holes in the slapper and one in the guy with the shotgun. Then he slammed it shut as a volley of lead shredded the outside. Hugging the wall, he went to a window, he glanced out. The thugs had taken up positions behind the vehicles. He peered again and saw one moving left to flank him and come in through the kitchen or a backside window. If that happened, he'd be trapped. He took another look. Illiana was still on the ground, not moving. The old man was slumped in his wheelchair, twitching uncontrollably. Billy shook his head in despair. There's too many of 'em. I can't do it alone. Then a thought occurred, a very unusual thought, and he ran for the safety of the secret room.

Billy pulled the door of the safe room closed and rushed to the phone then dialed the three-digit number and said what needed to be said. Afterward, he paced the spongy floor. How long would it take for them to arrive? Minutes? Hours? Time dragged. His anxiety grew. His pace increased. Illiana was important. Too important to abandon to hope. He couldn't just stay in the safe room and wait. Without another thought, he undid the locks and pushed open the door. He listened, heard nothing, cautiously stepped into Vanko's office. Then he was in the hallway. Gliding up the stairs. At a bedroom window. Vanko's window. His window. He opened it a crack, just enough to get off a couple of rounds and put one or two down before the glass started flying. He was about to open fire when he heard the sirens. At the sound of them, the thugs froze. Their heads swivel toward Chipmunk Lane. The wailing became louder. Soon, Billy saw the first squad car roll up the drive, lights ablaze, a second behind it. They stopped where the road split into a circle, cruisers side by side, blocking the exit. The mob guys were in a dither. They couldn't keep their backs to the cops and didn't want to be a target for the gunner. Overall, the cops seemed a greater threat, so they skittered around the vehicles to the house side for protection. Billy thought it was hilarious—as well as an ideal opportunity to ventilate some punks—so he let go with three quick rounds and saw one man fall. Hearing the shots, the cops thought they were under fire and leaped from their cruisers, guns ablaze, peppering the van and limo with dozens of rounds. The mob guys returned fire. The cruisers' windows shattered and tires blew. Another heavy volley from the cops

caused the gas tank on the limo to explode, sending a ball
of flame forty feet in the air and incinerating one of the
goons. There were only two left. They were behind the
van. They were talking. All of a sudden, one grabbed the
handles on the wheelchair and began pushing it, the old
man twitching and alert. The second thug was behind the
first. They'd vowed to escape or go out in a blaze of glory.

The thug in front pushed the wheelchair at a reck-
less speed, around the van, across the drive and over the
front lawn toward the cops, using the old man as a human shield. The second thug ran behind him, firing as he
went. After thirty or forty more rounds, the cops stopped
shooting. They didn't want to chance hitting the old man.
The thugs were moving steadily forward, straight toward
the cops, the second thug blasting away with two guns.
One cop went down. Another grabbed his leg and limped
behind the cruiser. The mob guy kept firing. The wheelchair bounced wildly. The old man had a death grip on
the armrests. The cops had just called a retreat when they
stopped mid-step. A slender woman in a black dress was
running toward the mobsters from behind. She was holding a shotgun like a baseball bat. Fixated on the cops, the
thugs didn't sense her arrival. Illiana swung with all of
her might and one thug collapsed. Another looping swing
and the second thug let go of the wheelchair and fell to
the ground. Illiana dropped the gun and hurried around
the chair to the old man. He was slumped forward. There
was blood on the blanket. She waved her arms toward the
cops. *"Help me! Mister Vanko has been shot!"*

# Twenty-three

The newspaper reported the number of bullet holes as dozens. But not in the old man. The blood on his blanket was only splatter.

Late that night after hours of cops trudging through the property—as well as firemen dealing with the car fire and multiple EMS wagons hauling dead mobsters away—the castle sat dark and quiet. Earlier, two burly firemen carried the old man up the steps into the house. Before departing, they suggested a ramp would be handy. The last cop to leave, a rookie on cleanup, asked her if she'd be all right. With many of the front windows shot out, the house would be drafty. She told him not to worry. Zone heating. He gave her a nod of understanding. Home sweet home. Nothing like it. A minute later he was gone.

It was nearing 10:00 P.M. and Billy had been in the safe room for almost seven hours when he heard a faint click and the bookcase opened.

They sat in the kitchen with the door to the hallway shut to keep the heat in. The night was cold. The wheelchair with Zim in it was pushed snug against the table, a steaming bowl of clam chowder in front of him. Illiana fed him a spoonful and used a napkin to wipe the dribble from his chin.

"Minnesota not nice place," she said.

Billy had never been there and didn't know.

Illiana had changed from the black dress into jeans and a poofy white blouse. She pulled up a sleeve, showing him red dots. "Mosquitos."

Billy nodded, glad she was back.

"Zim friends not nice either."

Didn't surprise him. Zim had told him their nicknames were Pruno and Shank. A guy didn't get a nickname for nothing. Pruno would be a drinker. Shank would be a problem. "What happened?"

"First, all good. Zim generous, give money, pay for party. All laugh and tell joke like friend. Days go by. Shank ask many question. Keep Zim high all time so not think. I keep close watch. See Shank go in Zim suitcase. Find money. Put in pocket. Afterward, mood change. Shank is acting like boss. Strut around. Make sex talk to me like I am whore. Beat Zim bad when try to defend."

Billy's jaw clenched and a vein bulged in his throat. He stormed to the drawer for the Glock. "Gimme the address. I'm goin' for a ride."

Illiana smiled. "Is nice thought, Billy, but not necessary. Shank had bad knife accident. Pruno run away."

Billy relaxed a little. "Wish I'd been there."

"Would have been good, lover boy. Knife accident

took long time. Shank apologize much, but did not seem sincere. I let Zim watch so he not feel bad about beating, but even clever knife work did not cheer him like should. Need care and rest. Is big job. Must find someone to help look after."

"He looks like an old man," said Billy.

"Yes, but has worked out good." She grinned. "I tell cops he is old man Vanko. They not know different. Said had stroke. Cannot talk. I say old man not danger to anyone, but mob want dead. That why they come. Cops understand. They all happy from fun killing of mobsters and not ask question about anything else. Maybe not even come back."

"Not come back?" Billy was on cloud nine.

Illiana shook her head. "And Gregor Bulnik is in Loon Haven morgue next to goons. Since police did shooting, no one come for revenge."

"No mob and no cops? Wow!"

"Yes, wow."

"I missed you, baby. I'm glad you're back. Stay with me. We'll take care of Zimmy. He'll get better. Then, if you still want, we can leave."

Her face registered surprise. "You would leave castle if I ask?"

"Yes."

She gazed at him. "What has changed?"

"Had time to think. Realized it's not a castle if you're not in it."

She rose and went to him. "You are sweetest man I ever meet. I never leave you, Billy, never again."

They embraced, but just before their lips met they

heard the *rap, rap, rap* of the knocker. Zim began twitching. Illiana calmed him by rubbing his head. "Billy, you go in safe room. I will answer door."

"Nah," he said. "No more hiding."

"Then we go together."

The woman in the doorway had big hair, bigger boobs, a freakishly tiny waist and dinosaur thighs. She was wearing a skintight leopard bodysuit with a wide white belt and matching heels. Her flame-red fingernails were an inch long. She smiled, wiggled, smiled. "Zimmy home? Tell him it's Lolly. That's short for lollypop. Tell him I got another job for the Squid." She wiggled again. Gave Illiana a wink. "And tell him I could use a little lovin'."

"You are friend of Zim?" queried Illiana, amused.

Lolly nodded. "Um-hmm. Got him the Crowbar hit." Her eyelashes fluttered like black-winged butterflies.

Illiana smiled.

Billy flexed his fingers.

Lolly's brow furrowed. She took a step back, eyes roaming from side to side, surveying the damage to the front of the house. Her lips pursed in concern. "Can't help but notice you've been under attack. Does that happen often?"

"No too often," said Illiana.

"Would you like a pepperoni and salami sandwich?" asked Billy.

Lolly smiled. Billy smiled back. Illiana smiled too.

# Acknowledgements

A huge thank you to Jim Simmons, Dennis Bell, Chris Kitzman, Linda Radmacher, Joanne Spurr, and K.C. Meadows for their help in preparing the manuscript for publication. As always, to Whitley, Maclain, and Katherine for their patience and understanding.

by Alan Robertson

The Money Belt

Diamond

Sierra Joe 9

Lila

Man's Work

The Rogue

Summer Moon

CPSIA information can be obtained at www.ICGtesting.com
Printed in the USA
BVOW02s2050050115

382042BV00001B/10/P

9 781478 733539